Heavens to

Murgatroyd!

stories & poems

ISBN 978-1-989642-50-4 (paperback)
ISBN 978-1-989642-51-1 (ebook)

Heavens to Murgatroyd: short stories & poems. © 2025 Shawn L. Bird, editor. Salmon Arm BC: Lintusen Press

These are works of fiction. Names, characters, businesses, places, events, locales, and incidents are either the products of the author's imagination or used in a fictitious manner. Any resemblance to actual persons, living or dead, or actual events is purely coincidental.

Original cover art by Nikolette Jones
Additional cover images from Canva Pro. Used with permission.

This book uses Canadian English.

Lintusen Press
PO Box 10019 Salmon Arm BC V1E 3B9

Heavens to Murgatroyd!

stories & poems

Shawn L. Bird

editor

LINTUSEN PRESS

Once upon a time,
on CBC's Canada Writes group,
a special poet bemoaned the fact
that she never finds her name in books.

A publisher said,
"Well, we can do something about that!"
and put out a call
for authors and poets to send in pieces
that included a character called Murgatroyd
to make an extra-special book
just for her.

And they did.

And it was good.

For
Murgatroyd,

of course.

CONTENTS

To The Universe   **9**
Shawn L. Bird

Murgatroyd and the Clerk   **10**
Robert Runté

Where Love Dwells   **17**
Renee Cronley

Chris Hemsworth   **19**
Trent Lewin

The Haecceity of Murgatroyd   **33**
Laurène Boutin

Guardian of Mount Murgatroyd   **36**
M. Gail Stelter

Murgatroyd and the AI   **39**
Robert Runté

The Most Murgatroyd of Misdirection   **51**
Donnalynn Rainey

Muskoka Mermaids   **59**
Lindsay Harrington

The Resiliency of Space Ants   **61**
T.L. Tomljanovic

Everywhere There Be Dragons   **62**
Lavinia Leon

67 **Out the Wrong Door**
Tom McCann

71 **Cuddle Me Outside**
Robyn Diner

75 **Adapted Management**
Alma Lee

78 **The Happiness Consultant**
Trevor Hodges

91 **In the Eyes of a Child**
Susan Duffield Lodge

97 **Delilah**
Sherry Cassells

98 **hyster/ia**
Zilla Jones

112 **Aunt Ida's Apple Tree**
Shawn L. Bird

121 **A New Earth**
Finnian Burnett

127 **Unbridled**
Janet Richards

128 **Author Biographies**

TO THE UNIVERSE

Shawn L. Bird

(For Murg)

From this dark place,
sending you space
for love and gratitude,
supportive attitudes,
help where it's needed,
concerns that are heeded.
Sending love and grace
to that dark place

MURGATROYD AND THE CLERK
Robert Runté

Enroute to *Proxima Centauri b*

The clerk said, "Next" without looking up from his screen.

Murgatroyd stepped over the line that said, "Wait here" and approached the counter.

The clerk, still focused on passing a memory slip from his previous transactions through the read/write slot, said, "Howcanwehelpyoutoday?"

"Replacement card." She smiled tentatively, though he still hadn't actually glanced up at her.

He flicked his finger across the screen to select a new page. "Lost or stolen?" he asked.

"Dropped down the crack between the floor and the elevator," she said.

He did look up at that. "That's more common than one would think," he said. "Let me guess: the hundred and eleventh floor?"

"I think it was sixty-eight. Basics."

His head nodded fractionally in acknowledgement. "It's usually hundred and eleventh, though. The maté station's right next to the elevators. People still have their tapcards out as they turn to catch the elevator." He mimed the scenario as he described it. "They're holding the maté in their left hand, balancing their snacks in their right as they're still trying to get their card back into their jumper pocket. And the elevator comes, they're rushing to catch it, then . . ." He sighed. "I keep telling them: 'You have to move the maté station another three metres up the corridor.' But nobody listens."

Murgatroyd's smile remained frozen as she tried to convey both commiseration with the problems the maté station presented for him and her hopefulness that he could help her.

"Number?" he asked, turning to the task at hand.

"I don't have one," she said.

He looked at her, askance.

"You're supposed to have it memorized." His expression said that people who hadn't bothered to memorize theirs were even more annoying than elevator-side maté stations.

"No," she explained. "I just don't have one." She raised her sleeve to show there was no tattoo.

His hand shot out and grabbed her wrist and yanked her arm over the counter. His other hand raised her sleeve again as his thumb rubbed across where he thought the scan-code should be.

"Hmm," he muttered when nothing rubbed off.

He let go and looked at her closely. "But you're a clone, though? Right?"

"No?" Murgatroyd said, though it came out more tentatively than she might have wished. She messaged her wrist where he had grabbed it.

"I mean, no offense, but you absolutely look like an M series."

She shrugging vaguely.

"Very well. Your name then?"

"Murgatroyd."

"An 'M' name."

"Lots of people have 'M' names," Murgatroyd protested.

"Is that your first or last name?"

"Just Murgatroyd."

His head tilted as he regarded her again, his expression dubious. He sighed. There were some cultures that only used one name, so there was a drop-down menu that changed "last" to "both", but it was easier to type in "Murgatroyd Murgatroyd" than search for the menu. He hit "enter".

"Oh! There *is* an entry!"

Murgatroyd tried not to reveal her surprise. She wondered if some fan had taken pity on her and created an entry for her—or if it was the name of an M Series.

"You can't show me your tapcard, obviously, so I'll have to confirm your identity with a few questions from your record."

Murgatroyd nodded.

"Occupation?"

"Poet."

"That's not an occupation."

"It is."

"I mean, what do you do for money?"

"Read poetry?' His head titled further, so she tried to explain. "I mean, read it out loud. In public. Speaking it. At cafés and such."

He straightened up. "That's *not* what it says on the form."

"What does say?"

"Odd jobs."

"Well . . . 'poet' is one of the odder jobs, isn't it?"

He rolled his eyes. "Alright, let's try another. Address?"

"I'm currently between apartments."

"Your previous address, then?"

"20-4559, West Elevators"

"I happen to know the 20th floor West is closed for renovations."

"Why I'm currently—"

"—between apartments," he finished for her. His head wobbled a bit: half nod, half negation. "No employer, per se, obviously. Digital address?"

"Oh, I have that. Murgatroyd5512."

"Excellent. That's a match. We just need one more. How about Embarkation Date?"

"Um, no. I was born aboard."

"Date of debottling, then?"

"Born. I'm not a clone."

"Having babies in transit isn't allowed. It's unsafe."

"And yet, here I am." She held up her hand to forestall his next comment. "Not everybody complies with regulations, but that's not on me."

"Okay, but—how do I put this delicately? Is it possible that someone *told* you were born, but really...you know... M class?"

Murgatroyd found herself grinding her teeth behind her

13

smile.

He sighed. "Look, I really am trying to help. But I can't just give you a tapcard, with access to all that entails, without at least some minimal identification."

"Retinal scan? Finger print? DNA?"

Another sigh, this time exasperated. "As you must know perfectly well, the biometrics bank is currently down. Otherwise, we'd have started there. You must use something to identify yourself."

"Yeah," she said. "The *tapcard*."

He closed his eyes, as if pained.

He opened them again and held up his finger indicating he'd thought of something. He flipped through pages on his screen. Paused. Flipped some more. Paused longer. He cleared his throat.

"You're Murgatroyd the Poet, right."

"I guess."

"Right, then. In the poem, 'Nightfall', what is the third word in the fifteenth line?"

Murgatroyd blinked, thought about the last time she had performed 'Nightfall', pictured herself under the pickup mike in the blackbox theatre, felt the heat of the lights on her face as she had pushed her hair back, and replayed the memory of reciting it. She ticked off the words on her fingers as they ran through her head until she got to the third word in the fifteenth line.

"Personhood".

"And the second to last line in "How it Ends?""

She was on the stool in the Express Café, two dozen two-person tables with the chairs all pushed round to the side facing her, the regular lights on, as people clinked silverware and plates and cups through the evening meal.

"I die a little, and then . . . "

And the fortieth line of "Rasputin Comes to Visit?"

Main Hall, a sea of nearly 2,500 faces starring at her expectantly, a poem she's read a hundred times before, momentarily stuck in her throat. That had been a big night, and a long poem. She pounded through it in her head.

"It's the Russian beard that does it."

He looked up from the screen, beaming. "I'm convinced."

He pulled a blank from a box under the counter, made a production of swiping it through the activator. A few clicks on screen, a tap, and he presented the card to her with a flourish.

"Linked to your accounts. You're all set."

"Thank you."

She tried to think of how to say she appreciated his taking…initiative. His humanity. Without acknowledging out loud that she knew he had violated procedure. That this should not have worked out for her.

"Thank you. Really."

He acknowledged what she meant with a gracious titled nod of his head.

She turned away, then stopped. Turned back.

"So . . . it didn't seem reasonable to you that anyone else might have memorized one or more of my poems?"

He shrugged. "Oh, one of, maybe. But getting all three, randomly chosen poems word perfect? I don't know anyone who even has three William Shakespeare poems down. Or Shane Koyczan's." He sighed, again. "Recitation becomes a lost art when you can simply request a playlist out of the air."

"I guess. Live is better, though."

WHERE LOVE DWELLS

Renee Cronley

She turns herself inside out—
heart muscle first, to hold up
the four walls that shelter
the best parts of her.

Despite the cold, she blazes on
with enough heat to keep
her children warm.
She snuggles them
with stories and smiles—
the room still saturated
with the comforting smells
of bacon, eggs, and pancakes,
whispering
of the love and laughter
that had filled their morning.

But the roof still weeps,
and the weight of its sorrow
is a burden she can't lift
with only two hands.
Her worries burrow and gnaw

through the drywall and plaster.
And the floor tiles are treacherous
because they keep turning into eggshells.

But Murgatroyd knows
that a mother's love
is the most powerful disinfectant.
She frees her hands to hold theirs,
and leads them into the wide world.
The fresh air is scented
with the promise of new beginnings.
And as they walk side-by-side,
the sun's warmth feels like a gentle hug,
and the soft, even ground cushions their steps.

She gives them a snuggle, a story, and a smile
        whispering
of a love that will never change.
So that they know
that whenever they are together,
they are home.

CHRIS HEMSWORTH

Trent Lewin

Before we had law, we didn't have a word for crime.

There are three in the crew: Murg, Mohammad, and me. We're not criminals. But we're not the law, either.

"We need a fourth," I tell them, over beer at the café.

"I got one coming," says Murg.

Mohammad groans. It's what he does before he speaks. "Three is good."

"We need a fourth," I repeat.

We drink beer. A fast train slides into the station behind the café. A plastic tub of margarine rattles its way to the kitchen. Below the shop, a basement of dirt walls holds a hammock, should anyone be so tired from the work that they need a nap.

You'd think in beer, you could find a dream. A true idea of what a human being could do with their life, but all I find is a crime that I want to do. It's been with me for years. It's with Murg and Mohammad, too, a niche-dream shared by a few people in the world, all the more powerful because of it. Especially when those who partake in the dream gather in Rome and drink beer at a café, to discuss the need for a fourth.

Of all the things you could build near the France-Switzerland border, a roadside petting zoo is the least obvious. There are three pigs, two goats, several ducks, no dogs. The D884 slices through

France and takes a hard right turn at Switzerland, crossing the border as though its hair is on fire. On that stretch, a man named D'Averc waves at cars that pass the zoo, beckoning them to stop.

Every morning, he walks the highway east towards Geneva and sees the Institute, a large swath of buildings housing thousands of scientists. They never stop at his zoo. Twice in five years, he's brought his animals to the Institute, at the request of its Director, a thin old woman who surely feels for his meagre business as she drives past his place on the way to work. He set up in a courtyard. Scientists asked if they could pet the animals. Of course, he said. Like this.

A car stops, and a family emerges. German. On their way to the Institute to take a tour and make understanding of the brilliant science. "Do you think they could actually make a black hole and destroy everything?" asks the woman.

"His name is Petri," D'Averc says of a goat.

"I heard that unstable people across the world come to CERN because of the collider," says the man. "The particles crashing together, it calls to them. Have you seen any unstable people?"

"Now this is Estelle," D'Averc continues, bringing out a pig. The children, a boy and a girl, go to the animal. "Her old owner used to let children ride her, but I don't allow it. You can pet her, though. Like this."

"What do you do with a pig when it dies?" asks the little girl.

"I bury it," lies D'Averc.

A dare. It's what Murg does. Her eyes, her posture, her lean legs: they dare you. They dare the unthinkable, a life together, children, growing old in the countryside.

"We have a fourth," she says.

Mohammad puts down his phone. Murg brings in a tall man with blue eyes and whose curly blond hair sneaks from the edges of a hoodie. He's wearing a mask.

"I'm Allyn," I tell him. "That's Mohammad. Can you tell us why you're interested in this?" Are you one of us? "This is risky. If we get caught, we'll be in jail." When did you first have a dream of this crime? "No one has ever tried this before." Did something call to your imbalance, to come here, to answer Murg's post, to navigate towards the three of us, to be our fourth?

He puts his hood down and takes off the mask.

"Jesus," grunts Mohammad. "You're Chris Hemsworth."

"Not right now," he says. "I'm between jobs."

I pull close to Murg. "He's a movie star."

"He answered the ad."

"He's not covert."

"He gets the mission. He's one of us." Dark eyes flash. They dare.

"We can't move around freely if we're with Chris Hemsworth."

"I have a hoodie and a mask" says the man, putting on his disguise. As though by magic, he's just a tall man again. "When do we get started? I'm excited."

We stand there. I shake the hand of our fourth. It's strong and fierce, and his eyes look at me as though trying to figure out how serious I am about this crime. I squeeze back, letting him know that I was first in this group. The original.

Summer is limoncello in the afternoons until the correct time for barolo. We go into Rome with hoodies and masks. I am so interested in CERN, Chris Hemsworth tells us. Have been since I was a kid. I even tried to get a movie made about it, so that I could spend time there. We ask him about the *Avengers* nonsense, and he laughs, says he got lucky with that, and that Chris Evans is a truly nice guy.

We go to a ball pit for adults, the plastic balls as large as grapefruits. They give us forty-five minutes alone in there, mirrors on every wall, the lighting low. There is a song playing, an 80s remake. We take off our hoodies, dive. It's deep, this ball pit. It's easy to sink. When you move your arms, you can swim. Now and then, I touch another human being. It's a glancing blow, and like a squeamish fish, the limb retracts. On the other side of the pit, Murg and Chris are standing on the wall. They plug their noses and jump. The balls swallow them, but we can see the wake of their movement as they swim.

Mostly, we train. We have plans of CERN, specifically the Large Hadron Collider that people once thought would smash atoms so forcefully that the twenty-seven-kilometre ring would initiate a black hole. We understand the security situation. We know the scientists responsible for doing experiments. We practice our infiltration and our escape. We put on our outfits, to make sure they are perfect. We refine our identification badges and practice our fake names.

"Holt Soutenir," says Chris. "That's what I want to be called."

We don't argue. When it comes time to buy a van, Chris pays for it in cash. We thank him by making lasagna. When it's time to disconnect from our network, we put our phones in a plastic bag, toss a brick in it, and throw the lot into the Mediterranean. In the distance, a super-yacht looks like it was drawn by crayons. On the deck, a young man is doing yoga. Are you a criminal, too, I want to ask him, as he bends backwards in the sunshine?

On Monday, D'Averc finds Estelle dead in her pen, her sides gutted.

"Wolf," he says into a telephone. "From the mountains." The voice on the other end says they can't do anything about a wolf, even if one did come this far west.

That night, he stays outside and watches the pens. He has a

22

slingshot ready, no gun. Guns are easy in Switzerland. If he wanted, he could get an automatic and fire it at will into the dark country, but D'Averc has had enough of guns. The slingshot is a toy, but he tests the bands and flings rocks at targets with tremendous force.

Near three in the morning, he falls asleep. An hour later, he hears growling. There is a shadow in the pen with Petri, the goat that no longer has a head.

D'Averc reaches for a rock, loads his slingshot, fires. He runs towards the pen, firing from a stockpile of rocks in his pocket. Then he stops. White, glowing eyes stare at him, the eyes of a wolf, but they are brighter than they should be. The beast is bigger than he imagined. It stares at him as it chews on Petri.

D'Averc edges back towards the house. The rest of the night, he stands behind a window, watching the pens. By morning, the wolf is gone, and of Petri, there is nothing left.

"Murg asked me something," says Chris, in the passenger seat. They have left Italy and are driving west through France.

"Murgatroyd."

"What?"

"That's her full name."

"Fine, fine. She asked me how this crime could be more interesting than being in a movie. I told her that what you see in a story like that takes a lot longer to make than the story you see. It's a job. This isn't a job. That's what I told her."

My first dream of a black hole was when I was five. I was staring at the moon, and just to the side of it, a black hole appeared. It was coming closer, as though it had just entered the solar system, all of us unwarned and unaware. I rubbed my eyes, but it was still there. The second time, I saw one in my coffee cup. It was clear as a star, the light unable to escape the foam.

23

"We're not crazy," I tell him.

"Doesn't matter if we are."

Later, Mohammad sits next to me. "If we go to jail, we can write each other. Talk about our cellmates. Say all the things we never said when we were together."

"Like what?" I ask this bearded man with the bald spot.

"I could be an architect. I could be married. Have a skin condition and read comic books."

"That's a lot."

"And you?"

In a sub-basement of the digital world, I found a telling once, that humanity has only one job: to visit the end of all things. It's a video game. Once we press the button on the other end of that ending, everything will be plainer. Clearer. I've never been clear, I tell Mohammad, and he nods.

"I just want to push that button," I tell him.

"It's red, and clicks when you press it," he says.

Fire button, I think. We used to call it a fire button.

Two pigs, a goat, and several ducks. No dogs.

D'Averc makes space for them in the house. The pens are smaller, and the animals make a mess of his living room, but at least they're safe. During the day, three cars stopped to use the petting zoo. D'Averc brought them inside and showed the children how to pet the animals. Have you seen any crazy people on the way to CERN, a few of the adults asked him? Is that a thing? No sir. No ma'am. That's a rumour. A tourist story.

That night, he sits on the porch with his slingshot. He's had two wives in his life. One decided that she wanted to live in North America, and that he would be ill-suited to that climate. Bad for his health. He remembers telling her that he could try, but she'd been sure. The second woman had engaged him in conversation at a coffee shop. He remembers his head buzzing with caffeine as she'd told him about her scuba diving adventures. I don't scuba dive, he told her, but that hadn't mattered, at least not until later. She'd found a woman to spend her time with, and soon after, to spend her life with.

He sits on the porch alone. At two in the morning, he goes upstairs to bed. Alone.

An hour later, noises wake him up. He grabs the slingshot and runs down the steps. In the darkness of his living room, there are wraiths dancing like savages, drumbeats emanating from the jungle, back in a time when life was simplicity. There is blood. There are screams. Stop! he cries. He wades into the makeshift pens as the dance progresses, the cries. He locks his arms around a thick body in the middle of it and holds tight until it tosses him off and goes back to feasting.

He lies in a heap. When the morning comes, the ducks are gone. The remaining goat is gone, and one of the pigs. There is one pig left, Oscar. There is a hole in its hind leg that D'Averc patches up as best he can. They sit on the porch together, D'Averc kneading the flesh of the animal. The door behind him has been smashed.

A car turns into the driveway. Three children emerge with their parents, wanting to know if they can see the animals. There's only one left, he tells them, with Oscar in his lap. You can sit with me and pet him if you want.

What happened to your door? asks the mother.

A wind off the mountain, he tells them. It can be harsh. Are you going to CERN?

CERN? asks the father. What's that?

"Here we go," I tell everyone. Over the hill, CERN appears inside the great ring of the Large Hadron Collider. We're dressed in

25

construction gear, have iPads with work orders. We have toolboxes and a pipe wrench the size of an aircraft carrier.

At the security gate, the guard reviews our accreditations.

"He looks familiar," says the man, of Chris.

He's cut his hair and grown stubble to disguise himself. In a southern US drawl, he says, "Can I use your shitter, man?"

The guard shrugs. "Follow the orange arrows to the maintenance building. Check in there."

Murg lists our names in the ledger. Holt Soutenir. Suchat Leungspraat. Jennifer Plus-Vert. Chris Evanson.

"You better hurry," says the maintenance supervisor, behind him the spilled entrails of a massive robot overlord. "The collider's set to run. You have one hour, then have to clear out for the four-hour safety purge."

"It'll be close, mate," says Mohammad, in an Australian accent. "We have to make the place safe for the run."

"Just hurry up," says the man, vanishing into the robot guts.

It's inappropriate to high-five, but even still, I tell the team the obvious: "We're in."

Construction drawings show us which way to go. Along a hallway, through a control room, past another checkpoint where two women in white shirts are flicking rubber bands at a wall, through a doorway to stairs. My ears get stuffed as we go down. At the bottom, a long, circular hallway.

"This is the passageway around the collider," I tell them. Down the hallway, we find a service door into the collider itself. "Let's work."

The bolts are rigid, hard to start, but one-by-one, they pop out. It's half an hour until the safety purge.

"God this is a thrill!" says Chris.

When the door is free, we pull it off. Inside, there is a round tunnel like a subway that goes in circles; in the middle of it, a blue

26

snake that wraps along the curvature of the space. This is the collider, the vessel for the acceleration of particles, going so fast that people thought their collisions might create a black hole.

Murg snaps pictures. Mohammad puts his hands on the blue tube, with its hinges and flanges and access ports. On the walls, there are panels connected to instrumentation sticking into the blue tube, to monitor the organism.

"All right, let's finish," I tell them.

"Are you sure you don't want company?" asks Murg. "I can stay with you." It's a suggestion, an offer. A dare. I'm a criminal and she's unthinkable, and twice in my life, I saw a black hole. But only twice.

"Come get me after," I tell her.

Then they put the door back in place and bolt it. I turn to the blue tube. It doesn't make a sound. Doesn't look like anything. Down the hallway, there is an instrumentation panel. In the middle of it is a red button behind a plastic case. It looks like a taillight. A laser beam. It looks like magic.

We're in the van, driving away from the Institute.

"What happened?" asks Murg.

"Pull over on the other side of the hill," I tell them. I'm sweating. Breathing hard.

Mohammad drives fast. He finds a logging trail into a woods. The van slides to a stop. I take off my coveralls.

They stare at my right arm. It's bright. It's glowing. People would call it blue, but there's gold in there, too. I pick up a rock and close my hands around it, until it shimmers and shivers and becomes little bits of dust. I take another one and throw it, and it vanishes into the sky like it's never going to come down.

"Let me see," says Murg. She comes up to me, something she never does. Puts her hands on my glowing arm and squeezes the

27

flesh. "What does it feel like?" she asks.

"You're charged," says Mohammad. "The collider charged you, like a battery. What else can you do?"

"I don't know."

"How long do you think this will last?"

I shrug. Murg is still touching me. I'm not dying, I tell her. Don't treat this like it's an ending.

"I have a suggestion," says Chris. "Try this." He holds his arm up and makes a fist. "Now bring your arm down and pretend you're throwing your hand away."

As I try it, a flash of light comes from my fingers and soars at a clump of boulders to the side of the path. They shatter into dust.

"Nice one," he says. "Point your finger upwards. Just like that. Now thrust your hand at the sky."

A bolt of light soars, a white tower of fiery stuff that doesn't stop rising until I put my hand down.

"Okay," says Chris Hemsworth. "Okay, that's good. We can work with this." Chris grins. It's a wonderful smile, and the three of us stand there marvelling at the thing. We get in the van. They tell me that I don't have to drive. That I should sit in the back and relax. Murg stays near me, as the others sit up front and take us back to France. She stares at me the whole way, waiting for whatever comes next.

Night comes. The arm shines. Chris changes places with Murg and teaches me a few things. Make a claw and see what happens. Snap your fingers, that's a classic. You have to figure out your aim. This isn't like pulling a trigger. Move your hand fast enough, and you may open a portal.

Do you really believe that?

He gives me that movie star grin.

Later, Mohammad slams on the brakes. "What was that?"

"Animal," breathes Murg. "You clipped it. Pull over!"

They head down a driveway. There's an old house at the end. Outside, empty animal pens with a backdrop of mountains. The headlights illuminate an old man on the porch. When they get out, he points a slingshot at them.

"Easy, sir," says Mohammad. "We might have hit one of your animals."

"It's not mine," he says. "It's a wolf. A wolf from the mountains." His eyes fall on our fourth. "You're bloody Chris Hemsworth."

He shrugs, as though it doesn't matter.

"And you," he says, pointing at me. "Your eyes are glowing. How did that happen to you? It's just like the wolf. No normal wolf. It took down my door. I've only one pig left, Oscar. I've got him upstairs, in a closet, with a cupboard in front, but that's not going to stop this thing."

We hear a growl from the darkness. Against the black of the mountains, there are two white eyes watching us, leaving a trail of light as they move.

"Jesus," says Mohammad.

"That's not normal," says Chris.

I take off my coveralls as the eyes come closer. I point my fingers at the sky just like Chris taught me and pretend I'm flying. Light streaks skyward, lighting up the plain and the shape of the wolf as it comes closer. It's bigger than any wolf should be. Stands on two rear legs as claws point in our direction, and jaws snap.

"Looks hungry," says Chris, inching back with the others.

The wolf's running at us. Its eyes slide, as though deciding who to attack first. I put my fingers into a ball and release, sending a streak of light in its path, shattering the scrub. The wolf runs through it. I light up my hand and hit the ground, shaking the earth until we can barely keep our balance. But the wolf runs on.

I close my eyes. In the darkness above, a hole opens in space.

It swirls as it eats light, a portal or a path, I can't decide which, to a place I've never been. I had a dream of a black hole sliding into our solar system, gliding by on the way to a vacation resort on the other side of the galaxy. We all need a rest. We all need to escape. As the thought hits me, heat builds in my right arm. It builds so much that I'm a star, a human star on the scrub at the edge of everything and evermore.

I release a bolt of hot light at the wolf. It hits the creature mid-stride and sends it hurtling. The creature howls as it hits the ground. The lit eyes stare, but it doesn't get up.

Murg is running towards it.

"Don't!" cries the old man with the slingshot.

We find her with the animal. It's still alive but hurt, fur singed, skin black where it was hit. She's sitting next to it, holding a paw. "How do you feel?" she asks the animal. Her voice is low, like the rest of us don't exist. I wonder what she sees as she holds the beast, and it - it looks up at where the black hole is passing us by, a void of light that glows, an oddity of existence that needs a break. A stranger in the skies.

The next morning, the old man D'Averc lets us pet Oscar, Oscar with the hobbled leg. He's the cutest pig I've ever seen. Chris picks him up with both arms and holds the animal over his head, says he'll send the old man money to rebuild the petting zoo now that the wolf has gone back to the mountains. Are you criminals, asks the old man? No, I tell him. We're the cast in a film. Movie stars. We're astronauts, getting ready for a bit of travel. And we're atoms, smashing against each other all the time, connecting and flying apart, collisions that are catastrophes or victories, it depends. It really does. He tells me that he's been married twice in his life. Wishes us good luck as he holds the pig in his arms, like he's never going to let go.

The movie theatre is lit up. Murg, Mohammad and I sit near the front, in designated seats. Around us, beautiful people in beautiful clothes are pretending they're not special. They give each other hugs. They nod at us, trying to figure out if we're special, too.

My arm doesn't glow as much these days. It's hidden in a sweatshirt.

They did an investigation at CERN to figure out who damaged the Large Hadron Collider. They say that the vandalism could have created an incident, possibly an uncontrolled fusion reaction that may have damaged reality. They are exhausting all possibilities to find the culprits responsible, but the news cycle has become distracted. People are forgetting. Soon, the scientists return to smashing particles, to figure out what is emitted from those tiny, senseless collisions that no human has ever touched. Or so they think.

A director gets on stage and talks about the movie premiere. He had to consult with many scientists to properly portray the physics of a space elevator that gets hit by a meteorite and strands several people in orbit. No way to climb up. No way to come down. It's a hero's journey, he tells the audience.

Chris gets on stage and waves to the crowd. He smiles, not quite the way he did when he was with us. But it's a good smile. He points at the three of us and claps his hands, and everyone turns towards us, wondering who we are. He talks for a moment about his hiatus from movies, how it recalibrated what he looks for in a script, how he's no longer interested in tidy little tales with discernible conclusions. Life isn't like that, he explains to the audience. We don't know our conclusions, and so our stories shouldn't be so neat. As the crowd cheers, the lights dim, and Chris puts his hands together in thanks.

"I love that guy," says Mohammad.

I put my hand into the popcorn. We've been sitting so long that the bag is empty, except for the unpopped kernels at the bottom. I put my fingers around one of them and think about the size of the universe in which I live. Heat mounts at my fingertips. Once, I had a vision of a black hole sliding into our solar system. Like a photograph, it appears in my mind, and as it does, the kernel pops in my fingers. A few people hear it, and look over, but it's Murg who reaches into the bag and takes the kernel. She puts it in her mouth and stares at me, crunching. On the screen, far away, maybe in another galaxy, a movie starts.

THE HAECCEITY OF MURGATROYD

Laurène Boutin

In a kingdom ruled by a Norman king, sprog Murgatroyd dwelt inside a cottage amidst a mystical forest, whither she scratched upon the earth with sticks, etched upon stones with other stones, and traced upon water with her finger to an attentive audience of wizards and knights and queens that lived in her head, but alas, her magic was still weak and she hadn't yet learned to write, but it mattered little for the essence of her being – her haecceity – governed her ambitions and ere long, maiden Murgatroyd was reading before she could read, thus imagining herself the valiant crusader or the noble princess or the heroine who defends the nation, fodder for her ink and papyrus, with verbum that dropped in her head like manna falls from heaven, a magical deed indeed, and before she knew it, she had grown all up and espoused a knight – hail the knight – a gallant knight who sired many children, eccentric individuals, each of them engaged within their own mystical powers, and the Lady Murgatroyd reared them well, and though her thirst to indite remained unquenched, days were short and duties long, ergo she stowed her reflections and her transcripts – prose impregnated with neoteric ideas – (avant-garde for that epoch to be sure), in a teeming folio, for later, and she embarked upon a new path, therewith learning spells and charms gleaned from the books of magic found in a scriptorium, and whilst her knight in his shining armour was out knighting about, Murgatroyd applied her newfound knowledge of incantations to the mentorship of young'uns, how to read and write and converse in a foreign tongue, a skillful skill, you never know, functional whilst negotiating, at parleys, terms of truce between the armies, or whilst out crusading in the name of God with the multitudes from hither and thither– dialects outlandish, outcomes unpredicted – and so time marched as time does and years fattened decades and warriors and knights came home to lovers not called upon but dreamed of for eternities, and aging Murgatroyd was jocundly astonished for she hath not foreseen what her retirement would bring at eventide, with leisure to scribe, sundry places whence to think, and so many flavors of words for a quill dipped in ink, that gamboled on the lives of her characters, tales so poignant the moon blushed and the stars shimmered against the dark background of the cosmos, and the gods were pleased with Dame Murgatroyd, hence they plotted and proffered a writing tournament – refraining from magic the only rule by which to abide – that drew rhymesters and wordsmiths from dominions afar and opened a door that allowed for Murgatroyd's thoughts to flow on parchment, thoughts thought whilst occupied in the cookery or expanding time inside a tome, or outside, replenishing her soul in the apricity of cold days, the elder's mirthful pursuits of diversion – and the jury weighed the merits of her words and pronounced her victorious, and lo and behold, the populace rejoiced as they fed upon Murgatroyd's enchanting tales and poetries, remembering the erstwhile compositions of their beloved Marie de France, and they begged for more accounts of bravery and great courage, sooth or fancied, thus heralding the wordsmith's future musings of legend making; tales of valour, epics of heroic journeys, and elaborate histories that morphed, over time, into folklore and yarns, some with moral lessons for the younglings, others not, and at times, her scripts be adopted by earls and countesses who frivolously discussed, in idle times, their thoughts vis a vis the common people they read about but knew not, and all the while, Murgatroyd arched her body over her scribblers, endeavouring only to emancipate those stories that inhabited her soul, the nebulae of her imaginings, whither mirth and wrath and woes begged to be conquered and deconstructed and rearranged in the vernacular of the day, ere long occasioning minstrels to sing her magnificence and the citizens to spread her words generously imbued with metaphors and imageries, wherefore the spirited writer was revered – she, now a legend across the vast and prosperous land – and heaven bowed its head in admiration of lady Murgatroyd's exceptional haecceity.

GUARDIAN OF MOUNT MURGATROYD

M. Gail Stelter

Black, cold, hard lava rock as far as he could see. Off in the distance, Mount Murgatroyd seemed calm, or did she? Her plumes of off-white smoke with just a slight tinge of blue coasted against a bright blue sky and ocean backdrop. Did she look different this morning? Tom stood on his deck and pondered the majesty of his volcano. Murgatroyd was his treasure. For some thirty years, he watched her up close, from a distance, and through his binoculars. He recorded her bursts and blasts. For thirty years, he wrote about her in poems and prose.

The nearby villagers knew when Murgatroyd was erupting, Tom would warm and protect them. He would come down from his secluded, off-grid cabin and start the sirens.

"Heavens to Murgatroyd," said the village elders. "Tom is coming. All will be well."

They called him the Guardian of Mount Murgatroyd. He was respected and appreciated. Tom had his perfect hermit-writer lifestyle, and he also revelled in volcano watching and this bond with the locals.

Many outsiders also came to Mount Murgatroyd, and while Tom did not mind sharing Murgatroyd with the mindless tourists, he was often frustrated when he saw them venture too close.

They came in cars, RVs and tour buses. They brought their noisy children, barking dogs and fast food messes. Murgatroyd was one of nature's exalted gifts meant to be enjoyed by all. Tom often heard the visitors exclaim, "Wow, oh my, scary, beautiful" and, of course, "Heavens to Murgatroyd." Tom kept watch. He was the Guardian.

A new busload disembarked.

He spied a young family venturing away from the group out across the lava rocks. He glanced up at Murgatroyd. Her dark red base was growing, and orange flames were bouncing in the red. Oh my, he realized, today was different. He saw the rock spreading and the earth changing as hot mounds grew and mud flows oozed. He spotted a Lahar river of water and rocks.

He was immediately in warning mode, but he couldn't help but smirk when he heard himself say, "Heavens to Murgatroyd, her fury is on us."

The Guardian ran to his ATV and raced to the town. He startled the village into action with sirens that reached out across the valley and up and down the ocean shore. The tourists started their retreat. The townspeople prepared for what might come, ready to evacuate.

Everything would be fine.

Tom halted. The sudden memory of the young family exploring too close brought fear and panic. Would they hear the sirens? Would they escape the falling ash and flying volcanic rocks? Tom knew the direction they had gone. He had no choice. It was the right, the only, solution. He must go and find them. He was the Guardian.

The cold black rock morphed into mushy, smoking hot mounds as molten lava flowed beneath. Burning smells and the gases filled Tom's nostrils. Smoke choked his lungs and clouded his eyes. The Guardian understood that the black rock could give way at any moment. He pleaded with Murgatroyd to spare them, to show him the way. Finally, he saw the family up ahead, cowering behind a rock. He heard a child's whimper. He heard a mother's scream and rage.

"Why didn't we stay with the tour? Why do you always have to do it your way? Oh god, I love you. I love you."

"I love you. I am sorry."

An explosion, then another and another. The red-hot lava was flowing. The black rock gave way, and the young family disappeared. Tom cried out in anguish. Murgatroyd spewed lava high into the sky.

A volcano must do what it must do. Tom knew the end was near. Murgatroyd was meant to be his destiny. It was sublime as a strange spiritual contentment overtook him. Tom thought of the writings: his poems and stories of Murgatroyd. They would live on. His soul would live on.

Tom, the Guardian, lay down on the fire and said, "Goodbye, Murgatroyd. I have loved your glory and your power." He gasped, and with his final breath, he said, " Hello, Murgatroyd, now, we are one."

MURGATROYD AND THE AI

Robert Runté

Still enroute to *Proxima Centauri b*

"It's minimum hourly rate," the day supervisor said, a bit apologetically. "But not much happens on nightshift. Once you get everyone settled, the rest of the night is basically yours." She paused expectantly.

When Murgatroyd didn't say anything, she said, "I figured, you being a poet and all, that could be writing time." Another pause while she waited to see if Murgatroyd understood the beneficence being bestowed upon her. "It would be like you're getting paid minimum hourly to write. Poetry." The supervisor managed a tentative, conspiratorial smile. "While the AIs do the actual work, eh?"

Murgatroyd smiled appreciatively, though her teeth were gritted. Minimum hourly was not enough for her to live on, let alone support three kids. The new 'incentivized' economy was not working out for anyone not actual Crew. It was exhausting. Still, a way to stretch her reserves out a bit longer while she looked for something better.

"Which reminds me," the supervisor said. "I'd better show you where the AI overrides are."

She pulled out her key card and led the way to a locked

glass-fronted panel, which, when opened, revealed a bank of servers. "Top row's kitchen staff, maintenance, accounting, and such. Nothing for you there. Second row is medical, not that you're to meddle there either. Orange button to pause actions, red to stop." She closed the panel, tried the handle to make sure it had locked.

Murgatroyd held out her hand for the keycard.

"Oh, this stays with me. Regulations say you have to know where the AI overrides are, but there's nothing about giving you access. Sorry. Nothing personal. Last time I gave night shift a key, the girl switched medical over to do her class work. Nearly lost *my* job over it. So, no."

"But if there's an emergency?"

"There won't be. There never is."

"But if there were?"

The supervisor shrugged. "Break the glass. But better be a certifiable, life and death emergency, or the glass is coming out of your salary."

And with that, she left.

Out of consideration for the 'new girl', the day shift had put everyone to bed before end of shift. Murgatroyd's shift started at nine, but some of the more lucid residents were allowed to stay up to ten, even eleven, if they weren't making trouble. There were twelve tiny bedrooms, just large enough for a single bed, bedside table, two visitor chairs, and the AI helper's supply cabinet. Only five of the rooms were occupied. The supervisor had said six, but corrected herself when she remembered that Colonel Gathby had passed two

40

days previously. He had been a Mission Founder, and already old when the ship had left earth, so his passing had come as no surprise. "Sharp as a whip," the supervisor had explained, "but had spinal issues and Medical had needed the bed for acute cases, so shipped him up here to us."

The remaining five residents all had varying degrees of dementia. Four were elderly, one early onset. Earth had forwarded the treatment breakthroughs but those had come too late for anyone over 90, and they didn't have the components for the drug portion for the early onset case.

The Ward's job was just to keep them from harm. Murgatroyd had read up on dementia strategies while waiting for her interview, and thought she might be able to add 'calm' to that mandate.

As they were all abed at the moment, Murgatroyd accessed their medical files, quickly ascertained their medical needs: what meds, exercises, entertainments the AIs were supervising. These were Model As, simplified humanoid robots that would help a patient to the washroom, remind them to wipe, to wash their hands, to pull up their fly. Pleasant voices and painted smiles that never showed impatience or unnecessary hurry.

They gave Murgatroyd the serious creeps.

She was looking through the break-room cupboard for an unclaimed mug when she heard a disturbance. An elderly woman was halfway out of her bedroom door, tugging against her AI helper, which had hold of both her wrists and repeating, "sleep now...sleep now...sleep now" in an annoyingly pleasant voice.

"What's up, Dr DeBeers?" Murgatroyd asked walking briskly over. She tapped the pause button on the little robot's head, but of course it wasn't enabled: if a carer could pause the AI, so could a distraught patient.

"I left my tablet in the sitting room," the woman said, nodding in the direction of one of the plush chairs. "And this monster won't let me fetch it."

"It's not very bright, is it?" Murgatroyd said. "No worries. Let it get you back to bed and I'll bring your tablet to you."

Dr. DeBeers was never going to win against the relentless AI, so allowed herself to be led back to bed as Murgatroyd jogged over to the sitting room. The tablet was not in the chair indicated, or either of the nearby side tables, so Murgatroyd made a quick search of the entire room, the neighbouring coffee station, and the dining area, all to no avail. When she went to report the failure to Dr. DeBeers, she found the AI tucking her in.

"It's not my bedtime," Dr. DeBeers was protesting. "It's barely past nine."

"Sleep time," the little robot repeated.

"Can't you do something?" Dr. DeBeers demanded of Murgatroyd.

"Not yet," Murgatroyd admitted. "I'm new here. I'll figure something out for later."

"I just want my tablet," Dr. DeBeers complained. "I've a paper due, and I'm bloody well not going to sleep this early with a deadline looming on the article. Why can't I write for another couple of hours?"

Murgatroyd was about to confess her failure to locate the

tablet when she spotted one on the bedside table. "Is this it?" she asked, handing the tablet over the head of the AI.

"Oh dear. Yes! Thank you!" She looked a bit sheepish. "I'm so sorry, but I was sure I'd left it in the sitting room. Honestly, I'd forget my head if it weren't attached."

"No worries."

Murgatroyd was about to leave when she noticed the little robot reaching for Dr. Debeers' arm again, as the woman tapped to open her tablet. With sudden understanding she realized the AI was about to restrain Dr. DeBeers.

"Stop!"

"Sleep now," the AI insisted placidly.

"No restraints," Murgatroyd said, grabbing the plastic strip from the AI. "She's in bed. She simply wants to work on her tablet for a bit. She won't get out again."

"Sleep now," the AI said, reaching out to grab DeBeer's arm with a new restraint.

"The fuck!" Murgatroyd said.

DeBeers meanwhile was hitting the AI with her tablet and shouting at it that she was in bed, damn it, but bloody well going to do some work. The AI ignored her protests and attached her wrist to the bars of the hospital-style bed frame.

"Calm yourself," the robot said, ignoring the pounding its pause button was taking from the tablet. "Sleep now." It rolled around the bed to pull the railings up on that side and produced a second restraint strip. DeBeers started to weep with frustration as the smiling robot grabbed her second wrist.

Murgatroyd tried confiscating this new restraint, but the

robot pulled out another with one arm, while the other clamped onto Murgatroyd's shoulder and held her in place while it finished. Then, still holding Murgatroyd's shoulder, it hustled her out of the room, and stood guard in the doorway, its robot hands up, palms out, in a 'no go' configuration.

Murgatroyd pulled out her com and called the supervisor.

"Yes?" The supervisor's face on the tiny screen struggled not to show annoyance, but failed. "What is it?"

"How do I countermand the AI?"

The supervisor frowned. "Why would you do that? Just let them do their job."

"It's restrained Dr DeBeers for no reason. She wants to be on her tablet, but it's tied her hands to the rails."

The supervisor nodded slowly. "You're new. I realize what it can look like. But restraints are actually a very positive treatment. One can't have dementia patients wandering around unsupervised. Left unattended, they're a danger to themselves and others—".

"—But she's not wandering, she's in bed. She just wants to be on her tablet for a while. There is no danger with the bed rails up."

The supervisor sighed audibly. "I was *about* to say, restraints are part of regular care. The patients find it calming, comforting even, to be relieved of uncertainty. They often get it into their heads that they're supposed to be somewhere, that they've forgotten something, or are late for something, you see. But when they go to get up, the restraints reassure them that they are where they're supposed to be. However many times they forget where they

44

are and what they were doing—or in this case, not doing—the restraints are there to gently remind them."

"I'd hardly call them 'gentle' or 'calming'." Murgatroyd held her com screen out for a moment so the supervisor could see Dr. DeBeers frantically struggling against the restraints.

As Murgatroyd turned the screen back to herself, she caught the Supervisor rolling her eyes.

"You're new," the supervisor repeated. "Obviously, dementia patients can go through a variety of irrational emotions. There's no way to even know what they are reacting to. The restraints hold them safe while they tantrum or react to traumatic memories or whatever. . . She'll calm down eventually and go to sleep."

"It's obvious what Dr. DeBeers is reacting to! It's being tied down for no reason!"

Another audible sigh from the supervisor. "What's likely upsetting Joyce at the moment is your being in the room with her to no purpose. Leave, and I promise you, she will calm herself."

"Dr. DeBeers—"

"—And stop calling her 'Dr. DeBeers'. She hasn't been 'Dr. DeBeers' since before she came to us. She's just Joyce now."

Murgatroyd took a deep breath to stop from saying what she had been going to. She needed this job. Instead, she said as reasonably as she could, "Just tell me how to get the AI to back off. I'll sit with her while she's on the tablet. She will calm down and go to sleep much faster that way."

"And what about your other five—I mean four—patients

45

while you're sitting with her? You can't play favourites, you know."

"I assure you, I'll check on everyone before I sit down. And again every half hour. Or if I hear anything. It will be fine. No different than if I were sitting at reception or in the break room. I just need to know the basic override commands for the helpers."

"There are no verbal protocols for countermanding the AI. If staff could give orders to the helpers, so could a patient. There's only the over-ride on servers panel. And as I explained earlier, that's only for emergencies. You don't have a key, and I'm certainly *not* coming down there every time someone wants their tablet."

The supervisor seemed to realize she was getting a bit heated. She paused as if collecting herself, carefully put on her supportive-management smile.

"Just follow the protocols. Let the AI helpers do their jobs. You're only there because regulations require a human on shift. For emergencies. Fires or a hull breach or whatever. Everything will be fine. You don't have to do anything. Just go write your poetry."

The supervisor hung up.

Murgatroyd went and stood in front of the panel to the server cabinet. It was more than her job was worth to break the glass against orders; and the cost of replacing it would be twice what she would make on this shift.

Great. First day on night shift and she was actually going to end up poorer.

She stood there for several moments, listening to Dr.

DeBeers whimper, then brought up her com.

"Whisper to Nathan, 'Are you awake?'".

Nathan answered, "I'm awake."

"Did any of your art supplies survive from the last move?"

"Oils and mosaics," Nathan said. "I had to leave the dinosaur mosaic behind, but I kept my tools and supplies so I could start over when we were settled."

"Good. Bring your glass cutter to me, can you? And if you have any plain glass sheets."

"I only have the small sheets. The big ones wouldn't fit the moving pod."

"That's fine. Hurry?"

She went back to DeBeer's room, but the helper still blocked the doorway.

"Visitor hours are over," it said. "Please return to reception."

"I'm staff, you stupid machine." She proffered her ward ID.

"Patient Joyce is resting until Day Shift wake-up. All Readings are within acceptable parameters."

"Those readings aren't acceptable to me."

The AI did not reply.

Murgatroyd tried to push her way in, but the robot had anchored itself to the floor and could not be budged. She retreated back to the server cabinet.

Nathan arrived moments later.

"Can you cut the glass out of this panel, and replace it after, without it being obvious?"

Nathan shrugged. "Sure."

He took off his backpack, pulled out a suction cup and a glasscutter. "Piece of cake."

As soon as she had access, Murgatroyd deactivated the AI helper for Dr. DeBeer's room, pushed past the now inanimate robot, and released Joyce's left hand. Joyce immediately rolled over and started tugging at the restraint on her right wrist. Murgatroyd went round the bed while reassuring Joyce she was on the way, that she would release the second hand, that it was going to be okay.

Released, DeBeers sat up, hugging herself and rocking back and forth. Murgatroyd rubbed Joyce's shoulder until the rocking slowed.

"Tomorrow," Murgatroyd said quietly, "I'll make sure you have access to your tablet when you get to bed. I'm night shift now. It'll be okay, I promise."

Dr. DeBeer's nodded acknowledgement. "I'm fine. I just need a moment."

Murgatroyd handed Dr. DeBeer's her tablet.

Dr. DeBeer's took it, opened it, starred at the screen for several moments.

She frowned. "What was I working on?"

"Just some bedtime reading," Murgatroyd told her.

"I'm sure there was something. Specific."

"That was before you were . . . interrupted. Get a fresh start in the morning. Just something light now, for bedtime."

"Yes, you're right. I'm exhausted. I'll just . . ." She looked blankly at the screen.

"This one's good for bedtime," Murgatroyd said. She tapped a collection of silly dog reels, which opened to an adorable Havanese discovering a mirror. Then she puffed the pillows so DeBeers could lean back comfortably.

Calmer now, Joyce settled into the pillows.

Murgatroyd gave Joyce's arm another quick squeeze, then went to quickly check on the other residents, all of whom were sleeping, watched over by their AI helpers.

Satisfied things were as they should be, she marched back to the AI panel to restore Dr. DeBeer's AI before anyone discovered what she'd done. She was fairly certain the helper wouldn't interfere with DeBeer again, but the only way to be sure would be to reactive DeBeer's helper and see what happened. If it tried to restrain Joyce again, she'd leave it off until just before morning shift when the AI's programming would be for the client wake up routine. That might be cutting it close, because Nathan would have to put the glass back and disappear before anyone saw him.

She arrived back at the panel to find Nathan beaming proudly and the glass back in place. Crap! She hadn't thought to tell him to wait for her to turn the AI back on!

"I so sorry. I should have said. I need you to take the glass out again, so I can turn the AI back on before anyone sees what I've done."

Nathan beamed even brighter, if that were possible. He reached out a hand to tap the upper lefthand corner of the glass pane, which obligingly swung open while the panel stayed locked in place.

"Figured," Nathan said. "Hinged, rather than just glued back in."

Murgatroyd gathered Nathan into a long hug, then

pushed him back as she tried closing and opening the pane. Closed, the change was undetectable.

"Yeah," Murgatroyd said. "I think I can do this job for a while."

THE MOST MURGATROYD OF MISDIRECTS

Donnalynn Rainey

At this precise moment, Murgatroyd was approximately seven feet off the ground, approximately seven feet higher than she had ever intended to be in her lifetime. For Murgatroyd, this was quite the problem.

She assessed the situation. She often told others that you only required two things in life: quick thinking and cheese. The lack of cheese at this height had been noted, leaving her quick-thinking.

To be exact, there was no cheese, but there was a large talon wrapped around her waist and an uncomfortably close view of an owl's undercarriage- which smelled exactly as she had imagined. Some claim that owls are wise, but their smell suggests otherwise. Like wisdom had taken one whiff and then wisely fled in the other direction. A pungent blend of musty forest floor and wet socks.

Murgatroyd's whiskers twitched in indignation. This nonsense would not do, not on a Tuesday evening. Quite ridiculous, she thought, this will not stand. No, not at all.

"Excuse me," she squeaked to her captor, her tone carrying the confident authority of a mouse who had spent her formative years swindling local foxes at the poker table (which would be true). "Just where, young man. Are you planning on taking me?"

The owl, whose name so happened to be Sir Cornelius Archibald Feathersnatch—he had added the Sir himself, for a touch of distinction—ruffled his wings, and let out a small, disdainful hoot.

Cornelius was unaccustomed to his dinner making conversation. Whimpering noises were far more common, and frankly, he preferred that. Ignoring her, he flapped one strong, silent flap and soared forward.

He was secretly proud of the silence of that flap. He had spent countless hours practicing it in the barn when nobody was watching. Cornelius was a remarkably vain owl.

"I said excuse me," said Murgatroyd, "I shan't be so polite if you make me ask again."

Overall, owls do not care to converse with their prey (except for an owl who went by Timothy, he was exceptionally chatty, to the point that his prey would eventually expire from boredom. An unusual technique but most effective). Regular owls, however, had a limit to insolence from small creatures.

"You are a mouse?" Cornelius intoned in his gravest tone (another thing he had practiced, Cornelius was insufferable) "Then the situation is obvious, I would think. You are supper."

Murgatroyd indignantly pulled herself up, as best she could with an enormous claw clamped around her waist anyway. "Supper?" she repeated, bristling, "Supper?" "Sir! I may be a mouse, but I assure you, I am far more than supper."

Cornelius was slowly suspecting he had taken on a little more than he could chew—pun intended—but kept his focus on the barn up ahead rather than responding, Murgatroyd continued, undeterred.

"I am an explorer," she declared. "A philosopher, a teacher, a thinker, a dancer!" She paused, caught up in a memory, then continuing, "But that was only the once—and I needed the money." "All that to say, sir. I am far more than just supper." She pronounced the word supper with the disdain reserved for the uncle who only shows up on holidays and spends the entire time insisting the world was actually rhombus-shaped, but only if you tilted your head at an angle and squinted. It was a remarkable amount of disdain for one word. Murgatroyd was a mistress of tone.

Cornelius remained silent. He had discovered early in life that appearing wise was quite often a simple matter of saying nothing.

Murgatroyd, though, was already planning her next move. *He has claws, and I have whiskers*, she mused. *There must be a middle ground here.*

Thinking of the ground, Murgatroyd glanced down. She had heard that Barn Owls flew low to the ground, but when you are only a few inches long–not counting your tail–this wasn't as reassuring as it sounded. The ground loomed ominously.

Had the ground been able, it would have told you that it was most proud of its looming, a skill learned from generations of trees before it. Unfortunately, Murgatroyd, despite being exceptionally intelligent for a mouse, lacked a connection to the ever-thrumming mycelium network below her, thus preventing her full appreciation of the effort behind a good loom. Her focus was concentrated on suppressing her fear of landing. *It isn't the fall*, she reasoned. She was almost sure she would enjoy the adrenaline of the fall. *It's the landing that hurts.*

No, going down was not an option. The only way, Murgatroyd decided, is up.

She flexed her back paws experimentally, testing the owl's grip. It was tight, but there was a little wiggle room.

"You know," she said, striking a conversation."You got rather lucky this evening. Few owls get the pleasure of speaking with me. I'm rather famous on the ground."

Cornelius did not believe her for a second, but his curiosity got the better of him and, adopting his very grave and serious voice again so that she would be in no doubt that he was a very grave and serious bird, he responded, "Famous? How would a mouse be famous?"

It's important to note here that one thing Cornelius did not know about Murgatroyd when he scooped her up, was that she possessed exceptional observation skills. Arguably, not at the moment he had grabbed her, but in her defence, at that time she had been altogether focused on maneuvering a questionably gained piece of cheese into her burrow. A task that was demanding the concentration of a chess grandmaster, and an optimistic belief that physics was optional. Naturally, she had been preoccupied when Cornelius had spotted her.

Indeed, during this flight alone, she had already observed an incredibly suspicious magpie, an up-to-no-good fox, and a badger attempting what she could only call an interpretive dance in a patch of moonlight.

She had squirrelled those observations away in her brain for later. They were useless to her right now. What mattered was the owl himself. She had noted the tone of his voice, felt the subtle extra push of his wing when he tried to be silent, and she understood perfectly who he was. He was a most vain owl, and she could use that.

"Of course, a mouse can be famous! I, for one, am famous solely for my birth. I am, as a matter of fact,(here she paused for dramatic effect) a princess."

This was too much for Cornelius and he audibly scoffed, "A mouse," he laughed, "cannot be a princess".

"Yes," said Murgatroyd, with a new regal tone to her voice, "many species believe that. I would not have even mentioned it if I hadn't recognized I was being carried by nobility. You have a grace about you only the upper classes display."

Cornelius was many things -a creature of the night, a predator- but over and above everything, he was simply full of self-importance, and really rather stupid. He flexed his body with pride at Murgatroyd's comment, releasing his grip just the tiniest amount. It was all she needed.

With a swift twist of the body and an incredibly deft–even if she did say so herself–flick of her tail, Murgatroyd freed herself from the claw, running up the owl's legs, and, coming to rest on his back, nestling into his feathers.

"What is this?" hooted Cornelius, bewildered.

"This, sir," sniffed Murgatroyd, mustering as much fake aristocratic offence as she could, which just so happened to be a lot, "is where a princess belongs."

Cornelius ruffled his feathers. He recognized the sound of authority when he heard it and, without realising, smoothed his flight. He did not, however, recognise the sound of being royally tricked–a fact that suited Murgatroyd in her current position, which was perfectly, precariously, perched on the back of an owl.

"Now," said Murgatroyd, brushing imaginary dust from her fur in a most regal manner, "we may talk as equals."

Cornelius, far too confused by the turn of events, temporarily forgot his plans to eat the mouse that was at this moment making a fool of him. But somewhere, deep in the back of his predator's brain, ancient instincts and the souls of a million ill-fated rodents screamed, 'Dinner!' Pulling him back to his situation, he squeaked out, quite indignantly, "You are food!"

"Food?! Food!" Murgatroyd gasped in scandalised horror, similar to how a mouse would at the suggestion of serving mouldy cheese as gourmet. "Sir, an owl of your nobility would never eat raw rodents!"

Cornelius flapped another strong silent beat, thought for a second, then gave in, letting his ego take control, "Well, I do come from a long line of barn owls." he said, somehow making his grave voice an entire octave graver.

"Well, of course you do. That much is obvious," said

55

Murgatroyd, her voice now positively dripping with admiration. "Your wingspan alone suggests Taloncrest heritage. Do you know your lineage, sir?"

The thought of a Family Name had Cornelius puffing his feathers up like an expensive duvet. In his mind, he was already composing a far more regal and dignified hoot. Adjusting his flight again, this time to something he considered approaching majestic, he began to glide in a way that was smoother than an eel in a butter factory. Those late-morning practices in the barn now made sense. Of course, he was nobility; how could he be anything less?

Murgatroyd, observing his preening (remember she is incredibly observant), seized her moment. "All animal lineages have been documented by myself, alone, in the traditional books. I'm certain I have seen your family on the pages. Perhaps you know your book? The Book of the *Distinguished Union of Monarchic Birds*? We could look up your name and add your portrait. I am most positive you belong there".

This hit Cornelius in all the right places. He suddenly longed to see his face in that book. Knowing in his heart his portrait would outshine all the others, his vanity ran wildly ahead of his common sense, officially declaring itself independent from reason. His beak twitched with imaginary interviews. "Oh yes, it's quite normal for an owl of my standing within the Book of the *Distinguished Union of Monarchic Birds* to carry the Princess," he would humbly inform the assembled, fawning press of birds.

Murgatroyd cleared her throat, suggesting that Incredibly Important Royal Business was about to be discussed. "Sir," she intoned most regally again, "While your plumage does indeed give it away, formal recognition with the book would be ideal. Protocol, after all, demands a proper inspection of your credentials."

"Yes, of course," Cornelius preened. "There is always

protocol."

Murgatroyd nodded almost serenely. "Your wingspan measurements, the precise gloss of your feathers–all vital details! But alas," she sighed dramatically, "it is impossible to bring the Book to the skies. Tradition, of course." Cornelius nodded solemnly, as if ancient traditions were something he routinely contended with. "Quite so."

"I must be placed–undisturbed–on the ground to oversee this dignified process," Murgatroyd explained. "Only then can your rightful place in history be assured."

Still preoccupied with imagining interviews about his magnanimity towards rodents in his role as a noble owl, Cornelius flared his wingtips."It is proper" he muttered. Then he angled himself towards the ground, which, as it had been practicing for generations, was still very busy looming.

Moments later, with all the grace of the princess she claimed to be, Murgatroyd slid from his back and her paws touched down gently on the grass.

"Now," she said with a soft serenity, "let me just attend to the formalities", her face twitched with a mischievous smile as she turned.

Flashing back towards the owl, she dropped a curtsy. "Please wait here. Tradition does prevent you from knowing the Book's location until your formal confirmation. You of course understand."

Before Cornelius could hoot his understanding of such a sacred bureaucratic process, Murgatroyd–Princess of Nowhere, but armed with the confidence of Everywhere–slipped quietly away under a hawthorn bush, then, once quite out of sight, ran as fast as four paws could carry a mouse. She had cheese waiting for her at home, after all.

Meanwhile, Cornelius (self-styled Sir, but utterly convinced this was simply an oversight on the universe's behalf) continued to busy himself perfecting the dignified poses that would, in his mind, bring the masses to awe. A sharper mind—or even a moderately blunt one—might have paused to consider the rather unfortunate acronym of the *Distinguished Union of Monarchic Birds'* and smelled a mouse-shaped rat. But Cornelius was not given to pauses, reflections, or, indeed, smelling anything; mainly due to the ripeness of his undercarriage.

In actuality, it would take several weeks—and relentless teasing from his peers—before Cornelius would even begin to suspect he might have been outwitted by a mouse. He would only ever suspect though, whenever doubt dared to creep in to his mind, he would simply fall back on the incontrovertible argument of his wingspan, and the doubt would retreat, muttering darkly about how it had far better things to do anyway.

Meanwhile, the ground, with the patience only geography could muster, continued to perfect its loom, a skill it would master in another millennium. Of note, the badger that had been dancing in the moonlight- he achieved surprising acclaim as a mime: a most surprising career twist. In truth, he did dance daringly once in public. But he was young and had needed the money.

MUSKOKA MERMAIDS

Lindsay Harrington

Murgatroyd said she had never felt
the pulse of the ocean.
Had never become
weightless in its brine.
—Had barely swum at all.

Though she sometimes brought her children
to the sad scrap of beach
on the polluted lake of their northern town
but she'd never submerged
in those murky waters.

It was hard to believe
as she arced into the warm embrace
of the Muskoka River,
which moved so languidly
we mistook it for a pond.

Our bodies became a couplet
of poetry immersed in Canadian iconography
Twin mermaid queens with underwater kingdoms.
We coronated each other.
Donned crowns of pickerelweed.

No longer middle-aged, we frolicked and splashed.
Pinkie promised to meet again in the Atlantic.
Dig our feet deep into cake batter sand.
Frigid waves breaking over our bodies,
converting us to its limitlessness.

THE RESILIENCY OF SPACE ANTS

T.L. Tomljanovic

Coconut sunscreen pheromones and barbequed fish flood the off-world dome on Titan twitching the antennae of a swarm of soldiers joining together in a red tower arching towards giants who blot out the very sun, but brutish magnetic boots topple hundreds of rocket ship hitchhikers—no matter, they number in the thousands—and form again, pincers ready, attack until the enemy's skin pimples with poison and shrieks fill recycled air, synthehol rains down in a tsunami of foam flooding the colony, cradling survivors carrying them away on a tide of ammonia-rich waters to a new Murgatroyd of space of safety.

EVERYWHERE THERE BE DRAGONS

Lavinia Leon

"A dragon's journey begins with a single scale."
(Chinese proverb)

Ruxandra descends, a peridot sparkle carried by the breeze. She lands softly in the middle of the glade where distinguished dragons gather. "Thanks," she whispers to the Dragon of the Wind as she furls back her wings.

The Dragon of Clear Water smiles. "You've been flying a lot lately, Ruxandra."

The young dragon, still catching her breath, sends forth a bright jade plume.

"Yes, Clear Water, I wanted to be prepared for school."

The dragons laugh, each in a glowing hue of flame.

"We'll teach you that, too," says the Dragon of Lightning. "Let's meet your professor and the other two students. Hop on."

Lightning extends his tangerine and lime coloured wings. The grass under his wingtips trembles into a fleeting filigree of sparks. Ruxandra climbs on his back and breathes azure as Lightning soars, southbound.

They fly for a long time, the sun shifting above them, lakes and streams scintillating below them. Ruxandra's eyes follow the effulgent water ribbons, all in pursuit of a grand lake engulfing the horizon, more expansive than anything she's ever seen. At the end—or the beginning?—of one such ribbon shines a waterfall, nestled among a patch of sandstone cliffs. Nearby, a dazzling golden dragon awaits, wings unfurled.

The Dragon of the Setting Sun is flying in from the west, bringing two other young dragons. As Lightning and Setting Sun touch the ground, they greet one another and the golden dragon.

"Welcome back, Murgatroyd."

The golden one radiates joy. "It's good to see you again, Lightning, Setting Sun. And meet you all. You must be Ruxandra, Smaranda, and Sabin." Murgatroyd smiles.

Ruxandra's eyes blink wide. "You've been travelling with the Dragon of Echo! What did you learn from them?"

Murgatroyd smiles. "They showed me the power of resonance and how far it reaches, even beyond sound."

Days fly by as if still on the wings of Lightning. For now, the dragon school means walks through forests that resound with birdsong, lion roars, and snake hisses. Even the mosses rumble here, Murgatroyd tells them, the thrumming of life is everywhere, and dragons made it all. Someday, she says, the three young dragons will find their own powers and add them to this effervescence of the elements.

When mentor and mentees return from forest walks, retreating into the tranquility of a stalactite-adorned cave, Smaranda breathes crimson fire, just like her scales, and Sabin is settling into lavender hues.

Yet, Ruxandra's flames are undecided. One rainy evening, she sneaks out from the comfort of the cave into the thunder of the waterfall, trying to listen to the shrubs and ferns that sought their home on cliffs. She sighs at times, but the rain tramples her indigo breath-wisps. Soon after, Murgatroyd's golden light finds her, throwing swift shadows and just as quickly chasing them away.

They stand in silence for heartbeat after heartbeat. As the rain subsides, Ruxandra's voice grows clear.

"I don't know who I'm supposed to be. I'm afraid there isn't a single thing I can do right, Murg."

"Everyone knows and can do something, Rux. There's no right way."

"What if I'll be the first who can't do anything at all, in any way? I'll end up nameless."

Murgatroyd's eyes flicker.

"No dragon has ever been nameless, except for one. But he has lost his name."

Ruxandra shivers. "I've heard of The Hollow One. I don't want to be hollow, too."

"He had more powers than any other before him, and used them well for aeons. But he kept wanting more. He wanted them all, and built new magic meant to draw the others'. That's why Echo banished him so he can never be seen."

"Is that why you went to study with Echo? Because they overpowered Hollow?"

Murgatroyd hesitates to answer, if only for a moment. "Yes. We need to keep resonance alive."

That night, she tells all the young dragons more. Every generation faces The Hollow One. He tries to prey again and again, but the reverberations that travel through the world keep him at bay. "He will come after you. If you can listen carefully to what this world reveals – and to yourself – you will defeat him."

Ruxandra's words burst out in a kaleidoscope of plumes.

"What if we…can't hear ourselves? I thought that your scales can tell you who you are, but so many dragons' colours change…and sometimes even their fire is unpredictable."

"Who you are is on the inside," Murgatroyd whispers. "All of us carry the whole sky. Clouds and rain and all. That's why we change, just like the sky."

Smaranda's wings flutter. "How does anyone find their own sky?

"You can try to pick a cloud, any cloud, and see where it takes you. It might lead you into another one, into a storm, or melt into the sunlight, but it will still leave traces, crystals of song and flame."

"Does that mean that...colour is music?"

Sabin clicks his talons. "Everything is both—and more. Just different kinds of scales... If your fire wants to be colour, you can try to sing it."

In the silence that follows, the dragons' minds and hearts are singing.

The hum of sunrise fills the next morning's air, but a new whir grows heavy. As every stalactite begins to warble, Murgatroyd listens for the unmistakable.

"The Hollow One has heard us and he's here."

She rushes to the entrance. The young dragons follow, scales rattling, colours at their shrillest, Smaranda's crimson turned vermilion and Sabin's amethyst about as bright as diamonds. Ruxandra's shifting to metallic ruby. *Wrath. A shade of fear. A minor scale.* Her voice, distinct, inside and out. Note rising as she does into the sky, cloaked in scarlet fire. The sun is a red giant, but *it's on our side. It has to be.*

The world is turning into—or has always been—a giant loom, and Murgatroyd begins to set aquamarine flame warps. She's longing for what's been, will never or forever be; everything woven into one moment. Emerald. *All connected. We can't lose.*

Thunder is roaring all around them. The cliffs now wail with ferns aquiver, wilting. Ruxandra sings a rainbow, then another, all sweeping, braiding with the others'. Call and response and call again. Joy, anguish, freedom, loneliness. *All ours. We're not hollow.*

The voices of Clear Water, Lightning, Murgatroyd – steadfast, yet ever-louder. The thunder fades as dragons paint the sky.

The four are ready for their flight back to the glade. They leave the waterfall behind, until it's long gone, way below the clouds.

Ruxandra smiles. *Azure is gratitude.* She flies a little closer to Murgatroyd.

"I haven't dared to ask this of anyone. Do the other beings that share our world know that we're making everything in it?"

"Some do know, Rux. Some do."

OUT THE WRONG DOOR

Tom McCann

She went out the wrong door.

She was told it was going to be the wrong door but she didn't have time to find another door or the energy to fight her way back through the way she had come. "It is unfortunate" she mumbled as she barricaded the door, "that the future seers could not have been more specific."

As she finished propping the door with debris from the alleyway her muttering continued, "You mustn't go through the door, they said. Did they know about the damnable werecats chasing me through the building. I hate werecats as much as I hate them half-giving forward lookers"

As she turned away from the door, she paused in the shadows for a breadth to get a better sense of what was in front of her. As she moved through the dim light she briefly came into view. Her long dark green coat accentuated her height and camouflaged the abundance of weaponry strapped across her torso. Outside of her coat her wardrobe was almost exclusively black. She favored black market military clothes she matched with old world Terran boots that blended with her both her fashion sense and long stride-running gait. Her telekinetimorphic weapons, commonly known as TKMs, were strapped conveniently across her torso and her lower and upper back. The low profile of the TKMs made them the only safe thing to strap to her back. Everything else was too bulky and caused too many issues if she got knocked on her ass.

She was the only person she knew of who had mastered the use of telekinetimorphic weapons to the extent she had. In simplistic terms, if your mind was strong enough, one TKM hilt could provide you with anything between a broadsword and a butter knife. If your head was clear of purpose and strong enough of intent, you could change a blade style TKM into whatever pointy thing you needed. For the most part she had mastered six. Currently she was in love with a broad-axe one that she used sparingly, because of the extra mental energy the enormous blade took to control.

Her one nod to heritage weapons was a Smith & Wesson Model 29 with six inch barrel, a massive .44 Magnum. It is a very old museum piece that she'd liberated and updated. She was not overly fond of guns. Their noise attracted too much attention. There were moments, though, where stopping something was more important than stopping something quietly.

As she headed towards the mouth of the alley she reached down and mentally loosened the TKM holster holding the .44 caliber gun.

Being a "retrieval specialist" can be a difficult hustle, she often thought, but a girl has to do what a girl has to do. She often considered herself to have questionable morals, but unflinching standards. This current job, though, was certainly testing the boundaries of both.

Politicos were just about the worst people to work for. Their motivations could be hard to fathom and their justifications were murkier than side street puddle water. The criminal elements were easier to understand and they paid better, faster, and with fewer questions about her methods.

Of the four human constructed satellite moons orbiting the decaying earth, Hawking 3 was the one she disliked being on the most. Chandrasekhar 1 (C1), Gaposchkin (G2) Hawking 3 (H3), and Lomonosov (L4) all were governed by the same entities at the top of the power structure. Each steel moon was designed to hold about 3.5 million inhabitants. All were their own small country of sorts, she just thought that H2 was the ickiest and ill-tempered the majority of time. She wasn't here by personal choice, but because of her choice of work. Now the job had been taken, it was time to get the hell off this orbiting scrap yard.

As she reached the mouth of the alley, her right hand went to the TKM-blade, and her left found comfort in the coolness of the Magnum. She paused and listened. She listened for all the things she could hear and all the things she didn't. Places like H3 had their own soundtrack, knowing what was missing had saved her life on more than one occasion so she took an extra breadth before setting out into the wider street.

Her path towards the loading dock was laid out in her mind: two lefts, a right, a couple of level drops before getting to the maze that is the main loading dock. Other smaller, more discreet loading docks could be accessed, but usually it was easier to sneak out of some place busy. Especially if you had the barter to grease the greaseable palms.

The shadows and murky layout made the lower decks the safer route for her to take. Even then it still took nearly thirty minutes to make her way to her shuttle and another five minutes scrutinizing the outer perimeter to make sure no unsavory types had been lurking about. The stories of shuttles being raided by lunar pirates had caused her preemptive lift off procedures to become significant and essential to her mental calm.

Her shuttle was an N-class Fillion, christened The Pomatter. Like its owner, it was fast, efficient and capable of producing a few surprises. Inside the Pomatter, more weaponry was squirrelled away than the physical dimensions would suggest was possible.

She didn't have an obsession with weapons, but if something bad was going to happen, she learned early in her life that delivering a bad day was significantly better than receiving a bad day.

She needed to swing past Gaposchkin (G2) before heading back to Old Earth to pick up the rest of her crew. Alone she was a force to be reckoned with. Backed up by the dysfunctional individuals that made up her crew, she was a true joy to behold in action. She was a lot of things to a lot of people but she thought of herself as Monaghan, Murgatroyd Monaghan, adventuresome retrieval specialist.

THE CUDDLE PARTY

Robyn Diner

I can't stop thinking about the cuddle party. It's being hyped on posters stapled to the wall of the old school Italian café at the corner of my street. A place owned by this guy Gio, who blasts Neil Diamond unironically, while serving lattes and craft beer to the kind of young people that move to Montréal to shop at overpriced fripperies and never learn French.

I keep asking myself: When did cuddle parties become a thing? Are they even really a thing? How do they work? Should I go?

The problem is I just turned fifty-two and would probably be better off spending Friday night at home, watching *Breaking Bad*—for the third time, or something. But maybe I'm wrong?

Back in the day, I would just go: go to the club, go to the rave, go to the sex party, go to the music fest, go to the dive bar happy hour. I hate to admit that I no longer feel at home in any of those places, that aging solo in the city is destabilizing, and that I really don't want to watch any more fucking *Breaking Bad*.

"Oh, just do it for the plot, Miss!" I can hear my Creative Writing college students urging me. They're good kids, smart kids, and they're not wrong. My life could use a new story or two.

When the night of the party finally comes around, I know I'm nervous because I can't decide what to wear. I skip makeup, since the new makeup mystifies me: all those layers designed to look like I've never heard the word Sephora. There's no way I can master that. I find a burgundy velvet flowy dress with a black corset, leather lace-up boots, a jewellery box full of silver chains and a long purple lace scarf that I stole from Urban Outfitters, because their prices are stupid. The look screams: What happened when Stevie Nicks met early-Madonna for brunch in Janis Joplin's closet? As always, I can't help noticing that all the anti-aging cream in the world refuses to live up to its job description. I lie to myself that it doesn't matter.

At the door to the party, two white twenty-something women with septum rings, Billie Eilish hair, and sneakers that probably cost $500 are taking tickets. They give me the most dismissive, "bonjour-hi," like I have too few piercings in all the wrong places. I'm ashamed at my urge to rage at them, to bolt back to my bed to watch all the Netflix in the world, to never go out again.

Instead, I fake a detached smile and take one of the flyers they're handing out, grateful for something to read. The flyer explains that tonight everybody's encouraged to ask anybody to cuddle. But if a person hears "no" or "stop" they are to back off immediately. "Failure to do so will result in eviction from the party." Fair enough, I think, wishing my generation grew up with a fraction of this respect for consent.

At first glance, the party's a Gen Z playground. So many tiny tattoos, oversized glasses, the baggiest of low waist jeans—and a girl wearing a pastel crop top that I once owned when I was eight. But the overall vibe is chill, as though nobody quite knows what we are doing here at this thing called a cuddle party. As I move towards the bar, I even spot quite a few older millennials. A non-binary bartender in tiger skin pajamas hands me a glass of sparkling white wine that I assume will taste awful, but it's surprisingly good.

I lean against the bar next to a mixed-race woman in her mid-30s with the most amazing corkscrew curls that spring up and

72

down to her shoulders. She's got a Star Trek baby-tee on, and there are peach daisies stitched into her black mini-skirt. I look down, delighted to see that she's wearing checkered Vans, as though her feet belong to a stoned skater boy. I tell her that I love everything about her look because I do. It also makes me feel better.

She tells me her name's Murgatroyd. There's Ontario in her voice, but also maybe Scotland. I sense she writes poems filled with wonder and rage, though as I go to ask her more, she disappears into the crowd. I lean back against the bar and perform looking casual, relieved when the hosts blow a whistle and shout, "*Que les câlins commencent*! Let the cuddles begin!"

A woman comes walking over and asks, in English, if I want to cuddle. She has a light Latinx accent that reminds me of a recent ex who used to do art, but now works sixty hours a week at an IT job he hates. "Yeah," I say out loud. "Hell yeah," To myself, I say "Thank you." I want to say it to her. But I don't.

Although she looks to be in her early forties, I sense she could still waste afternoons blowing bubbles off her balcony or shopping for the perfect pair of purple stockings in three different languages. Her thick black bob is the kind I could have maybe pulled off if my ancestors had been a different kind of Jewish. I already know I want to borrow all her clothes.

She points toward a corner of the room covered in orange and brown bean bags like the ones that overpopulated suburban rec rooms in the seventies. I follow her there; as she lies down on her side I surprise myself by snuggling right in, like a good little spoon who attends cuddle parties on the regular. She puts her arms around me. They feel strong. Yoga, I think, or Pilates, or something I don't do at the gym I overpay to rarely attend. I make a mental note to do gym things. She massages my arm gently. We both say nothing. My body starts to buzz, and my mind jumps to a

73

couple of current Bumble/Hinge/Tinder lovers that I sometimes invite into my home, lovers who make me happy when they both appear and disappear. But there is something about her newness, and this out-at-night-ness that feels so fucking good. It's a reward for stepping outside of the comfort zone that my aging self all too easily oozed into, and it's a reminder of what's still possible.

Too soon, the whistle blows to announce the end of the party. I want to ask the woman her name, to get her number, to follow her on any and all social media, forever. Or to Fiji. But that seems counter to the spirit of the event. Instead, I thank her and walk away delighted—like I just had the best first day of kindergarten.

ADAPTED MANAGEMENT

Alma Lee

"Cousin," I say, "you are not in a good way." I speak to him, half in English, half in our childhood language, not sure how much he still understands.

It is a strange thing to say to this cousin, who is really my brother in the messiest most twisted way possible. It is even stranger yet to tell a self-made guy, a multi- millionaire by latest count, to his face that he looks like shit. "You look like mooza-moo."

I say it lovingly, my real concern filling all the empty spaces of the words.

I get a laugh, not just any laugh, but the trademark snort-laugh. It makes me snort-laugh, spontaneous, immediate connection to the chorus of snort-pig sounds behind the backs of the priests and nuns at the school on the Rez.

We would start; everyone would join in so no one could be singled out. Instead, it went deliberately unnoticed, unacknowledged. Once in awhile, a new priest would turn, red faced and pissed, retribution denied by our faces, all innocence and meekness, practiced to perfection.

We gaze at each other. I put my palms flat on each side of his face. "Brother, tell me." I am gifted his tears.

My mom is his auntie. My father is his father. His mother is my auntie. We have history, big history. Big secrets.

Our father was Murgatroyd Monaghan, the man who instigated

the blockades of the CN rail lines, the Leader who defied the RCMP by shooting at them, unexpectedly hitting one in the arm, the face in the newspapers and on the TV, the man in Stony Mountain Penitentiary, the leader worshiped until he was beaten to death by guards. Officially, he was trying to escape.

Before all that, my auntie had my cousin, named after the father and gave him to my mother, who was pregnant with me. I was conceived, she told me, because Murgatroyd Monaghan was hiding out in the hunting cabin, and everyone thought Auntie had been killed, too. Her version of it all, "we comforted each other."

Together in Pearson International, we are just those confused kids, hanging on to each other like the old days.

"What we need is Sister Mary Perpetual."

We look at each other, instant agreement on a plan of action. One memorable year, we were in a split grade 7 and 8 class, together.The newest sacrificial nun, Sister Mary Perpetua, read out the class list. "Murgatroyd Monaghan."

"Present, Sister," the Murgatroyd, known as Troy to the school, replied politely.

Sister Perpetua fumbles a little, looking confused, frowning, "Monaghan Murgatroyd?"

I am Mona, to the school. My turn to answer sweetly, "Present."

Sister Perpetua looks at her silent class. Then, this new, young nun, in her best Snagglepuss imitation delivers the best line of our young lives: " Heavens! Two Murgatroyds!"

Sister had a devoted and eager class after that. She taught with as much love and humour as possible. She left us after that year, but not before she left her habit, convent, church, taking instead, the young Jesuit priest with her.

It was her final lesson. Freedom: grab it and go.

THE HAPPINESS CONSULTANT

Trevor Hodges

The airline had been referring to us as *customers* rather than passengers over the public address system on the plane from Los Angeles to Toronto; *hostages* would have been more accurate. After nineteen hours on three different flights and a six-hour stopover amid the chaos of LAX, I would have agreed to anything if they'd just let me lie down and sleep. Two years on from 9/11 and the security at Los Angeles airport was still crazy.

The international airport in Toronto was less hectic, but I did wonder who Lester B. Pearson was. They'd named the airport after him, so he probably crashed his plane heroically trying to cross the Rockies early last century or something. People with names like Lester used to do heroic things like that back then. There were yellow pieces of typing paper sticky-taped all around the arrivals hall, the word SARS in large black letters at the top of each page and instructions about how to avoid getting the virus below. So, our only defence against a deadly pandemic was a set of instructions on yellow typing paper? I wondered why they chose yellow paper.

"That"s the plane ticket," Alex said, placing it on the desk between us. Alex was my supervisor and he"d called me into the education district's head office to have this conversation face to face. "The flight's 6: 30 a.m. Wednesday morning. You'll be on it!"

"Canada? Really?" I replied.

"We've been through this on the phone, Doug. You're flying to Toronto to deliver a talk. Case closed!"

"But..."

"Not buts. The decision's out of my hands. Part of your Principal's employment agreement is that the Director of Education can require you to participate in promoting Departmental initiatives. Head office says either you go, or you're suspended. Without pay!"

"As if they'd suspend a principal who's improved his school's results by over 30% in three years!" I said, trying to sound more confident that I felt.

"Okay, but they could make your life very unpleasant; call you down to Sydney; put your school under review; send in the auditors."

"Ha! As if I have anything to worry about from being audited."

"They wouldn't send in that bloke you can distract by chatting about guitars and surfing. It'd be someone tough, from Sydney. Look, your school's results are a really good news story, why can't you just cooperate?"

"Why would the Yanks be interested in anything I have to say?"

"It's not just the Americans. Educators from all over the world want to hear how you dragged your results up by 30% in under three years. Word on the grapevine is the Canadians are particularly excited to hear you speak."

"Canadians are easily excited. They get all fruity when the temperature rises above zero. If I get SARS and die, I'm never going to speak to you again!"

"In that case I'll enjoy consoling your beautiful grieving widow. How is she... and the baby?"

"The *baby's* five and Susan is six months pregnant with twins."

"Wow, doesn't time fly?"

"Sir?"

"Huh?" I mumbled, coming back to the present.

"Welcome to Canada," the immigration official said, bringing a visa stamp down on my passport with a loud thump.

The heat washed over me like a wave the minute I walked out of the terminal's exit looking for a taxi. A digital sign showed the temperature was thirty-nine degrees Celsius. Wasn't Canada supposed to be cold? Yellow pieces of typing paper with SARS printed on them were blowing about in the hot wind like pandemic confetti. The hotel was a short taxi ride from the airport, and the lobby's décor was almost as jarring as the temperature. A riot of vibrant colours swam across the walls, fighting the swirling paisley design of the carpet. I walked to the reception counter humming "We All Live In A Yellow Submarine" to myself.

I'd been told I needed to register for the conference before going up to my room, so I left my suitcase at the hotel's check-in counter and went looking for the registration desk.

"Hall, Doug," I said, looking down at the two people seated behind a folding table.

"*The* Doug Hall? From Australia?" the woman said, looking up at me with a wide smile on her face.

"Ah, yes. I s'pose..."

"Lester! Doug Hall's arrived," she called to a tall man standing in a group of people a few metres away.

Lester broke off his conversation and walked over to me. He wore a wide grin and put his hand out, shaking mine enthusiastically.

"Well, isn't this is a real pleasure, eh? Doug Hall! We're all dying to hear you speak. Your talk is booked out. Well, it would be if most of the Americans hadn't cancelled at the last minute and decided to stay home."

"Cancelled?"

"SARS has 'em spooked. But we're not going to let a little thing like a global pandemic stop us, are we, eh?"

So Lesters still faced up to danger the way they used to. Lester B. Pearson probably said something like that before his plane went down over the Rockies or whatever it was he'd done to get an airport named after him.

"Welcome, Doug, welcome," Lester said, still pumping my hand. "Everyone, let me introduce Doug Hall! This man is an absolute hero... from Australia, eh!"

After much hand shaking, back slapping and congratulations from these total strangers, the woman who'd called Lester over shoved a sheaf of papers, an identity tag on a red and white lanyard, and a large white coffee mug into my hands. The mug was decorated with a red maple leaf on both sides, with "Two Rs International Literacy Conference 2003" printed around its base. I don't really remember getting to my room but the instant my head hit the pillow I was asleep.

I came awake and sat bolt upright in bed.

"Susan?" I spoke my wife"s name in the confusing darkness.

The glowing red numbers of the digital clock next to the bed read 3 a.m. so I lay down again, willing myself back to sleep. It was no use. My head, convinced it was 7 p.m., wasn't interested in sleep. I lay on the bed in the dark for another hour, but eventually got up and went into the bathroom. The face I saw in the mirror looked like my father's; if he had a hangover and hadn't shaved for a week. The hotel dining room opened for breakfast at five, so I decided to clean up and go down and wait. I took the maple leaf coffee mug with me.

I stepped out of the lift on the ground floor, walked through the Yellow Submarine landscape of the lobby and headed for the bistro. It was too early for food service, but there was coffee and tea available from a self-serve station, so I filled my mug with black, brewed coffee. I found a seat in a booth down the back, well away from the two other people sitting with their luggage waiting for breakfast.

I sipped my coffee and leaned against the high seatback, going over what I would say in my presentation later that day. Should I come clean and confess or keep my mouth shut and just make something up?

I heard a sob. It was a quiet, sniffy sob. And definitely female. There was a low groaning hiccup and a soft cough. Someone, a young female by the sound of it, was sobbing in the next booth. I'd heard lots of young females sobbing in my time as a school principal.

"Crying makes the eyes all puffy and red," I observed.

"Who cares when your life's over?" came the petulant reply.

"You're doing a remarkably good job of pretending to be alive, for someone who's dead."

"That's not what I meant!"

"Ah, so you were tending more to "life's not worth living" than "I'm dead"?"

"Yes."

"Glad we cleared that up."

She groan-giggled then sniffed. I hadn't looked around so had no idea whom I was speaking to, but our heads were only inches apart, separated by a row of wooden finials atop the backs of each booth. As I didn't see her when I sat down, she must have been slumped down or even lying on the seat.

"What makes someone in their twenties say her life's not worth living?"

"Eighteen."

"Stop avoiding the question," I replied, dropping effortlessly

81

into principal mode.

"It just is!" she replied, sounding more eight than eighteen.

"SARS got you down? Or maybe global warming has you questioning the future of humankind?"

"My dickhead father... who the hell are you, anyway? I don't have to answer questions from someone with a weird accent!"

"Weird accent indeed! What would your father say about you being so unwelcoming to a visitor from Australia?"

Another small giggle. No sniff this time.

"He'd say I shouldn't talk to strange men in hotels at 5 a.m."

"And he'd be correct. He's obviously smart and loves you very much."

"Huh!"

"So, why are you sitting in a hotel bistro at 5 a.m. telling a strange man your life's not worth living?"

A long pause.

"Dad wants me to go to university. Says my results are too good to waste. But I don't want to... not yet anyway. I want to try

"Don't tell me! I'd rather not know."

"Why not?"

"If you tell me I'll judge the choice, just like your father. Let's avoid the details and stick with the passion to be something, whatever that is. Okay?"

"Okay, I guess. You're... easy to talk to."

"I've had a lot of practice. Go on, without the detail."

"Dad wants me to go to university but I want to take a year off and try... something else. Something creative."

"Then it's no contest. You take your year and give it a shot. Preferably with his approval but if he won't give it, then without."

"But..."

"What?"

"What if it doesn't work out? Or I need more time? He'd so

82

enjoy seeing me face plant. It'd give him the chance to say *I told you so.*"

"Young lady—"

"Murgatroyd," she said, cutting in.

I paused for a beat, marvelling at her name.

"I don't think I've ever met a Murgatroyd before."

"It's my grandmother's name. Dad's mum."

"The only time I've ever heard…"

"Yeah I know, Snagglepuss said 'Heaven's to Murgatroyd!'" she said. "I've been tied to that stupid cartoon lion my whole life!"

"Then it's up to you to make your name, and you won't get to do that if you don't follow your own path. If Lester B. Pearson can do it so can you?"

"What's he got to do with it?"

"Well, he must have done something to get an airport named after him."

"He was prime minister and he won a Nobel Peace Prize."

"He didn't crash flying over the Rockies?"

"Not that I ever heard of."

"It's your *job* to face plant…Murgatroyd." I said, dragging the focus from her distinctive name back onto her life choices. "If you don't, that'll mean you're not taking any risks. You must take risks!"

"Do you take risks?"

"When I was your age? No. I followed the rules, did what I was told and have always regretted it. You get tied down so quickly and it narrows your choices. I've spent most of my life lining up and following the bloody rules."

"What did you want to be?"

"That's not important."

"There's nothing more important right now."

"The stage. I wanted to be an actor."

83

"What stopped you?"

"A lack of talent–and following my mother's advice. She wanted me to get a qualification first. 'Just get your degree,' she said, 'then you can do anything you like. After.'"

"There was no *after* was there?"

"No, and she knew there wouldn't be. I've spent the past fifteen years stuck in a job..."

I stumbled to a halt.

"A job you don't really like?"

"A job I sometimes hate."

I stood up and stepped around the end of the booth. I looked down at Murgatroyd and she sat staring up at me. She had a wild crop of dark hair, huge brown eyes and a half smile on her face.

"You've gotta take risks!" I said.

I turned and walked out of the bistro.

Mid-morning, I sat at a table in the central conference room waiting to deliver my talk. I had some slides prepared showing the reading and writing statistics from my school and a rough outline of the main topics I wanted to cover written out, but delivering the talk wasn't what I was thinking about. I was trying to decide what I was going to say about the only thing the audience would be interested in; how we'd achieved such a rapid improvement. I was also trying to decide how I was going to feed my family after I got sacked for admitting what my school and I had been up to.

There were lots of tables in the space, with seminar rooms leading off from the central area. Conference attendees, who weren't in one of the seminar rooms listening to the other speakers, stood in groups, chatting, or wandered around looking at the booths of education service providers, booksellers, and technology companies. I watched as a clown moved among the crowd engaging with different people. She would mime and indicate what she wanted them to do with actions then draw a coin from behind their ear or create an animal from thin, coloured balloons. Everyone she made contact with smiled and laughed at her antics.

A few minutes later I was standing in one of the seminar rooms in front of a large crowd. People from all over the world were there; leaders in the profession who would have no trouble sniffing out a fraud. It was time to confess.

"Good morning, folks. Look, before we get started, I think I need to own up to something. I've been at my little school, Bullen Burren Central School, for eight years. When I started at the school as principal, nothing we did seemed to change our results, even though we'd worked at it for *five solid years*. So we made some changes and started to see an improvement. I'll admit our results over the past few years are remarkable."

"You can say that again!" Lester called out from the middle of the room.

There was a ripple of laughter.

"Yes, we have had some improvement in our results," I said, pausing and swallowing. "But those results are all based on a lie."

Silence.

"My employer sent me here, probably in the expectation that I was going to tell you we got our results by rigorous testing and application of departmental literacy strategies blah blah blah. But, actually..."

"Come on, spit it out," Lester called out.

"Well, we did get these great results, but... it was because I ignored all the Department's advice and stopped my teachers following their policies. We basically threw out all the policies and started teaching reading and writing the way we believed would *actually* make a difference. All I did was give my teachers a license to teach the way we agreed would make that difference,

85

free from ideology and theory. I also told them I'd take the blame if the Department found out what we were doing."

More silence. Then Lester stood up, raised his hands and started clapping. Seconds later everyone was on their feet clapping and cheering. I looked out at their faces, utterly perplexed. Down the back, standing just inside the entry, was the clown. She was clapping too, although this time she wasn't miming.

After things died down, I made my way out to the central area and sat at the same table I'd been at before I'd gone in to make my "confession". I was trying to decide whether what had just happened was real or a figment of my sleep deprived brain. My confusion wasn't helped when I looked up and saw the clown standing in front of me. She didn"t say a word as she bent at the waist and stared intently into my eyes. Her face was covered in a thick layer of white grease paint and there was a small tear drawn under her left eye, her hair was a halo of bright orange. I looked into her big brown eyes and realised it was Murgatroyd under all that makeup. She winked at me when she realised I knew who she was and squirted a jet of water into my face from a fake flower on her bright yellow lapel. As I spluttered and wiped at the water dripping from my face she shoved a green balloon puppy into my hands then skipped off to annoy a group of conference delegates standing nearby. I looked down and saw she'd placed a business card on the table. It read:

Murgatroyd the Happiness Consultant
Available for parties, conferences, and weddings

I looked over at Murgatroyd as she pranced and mimed among the conference attendees. Everyone she approached brightened and laughed with delight. Grumpy, cynical me would have said I couldn't see much *consulting* happening, but all the cynicism seemed to have been drawn out of me, just for today.

At 5 a.m. the following morning I sat in the bistro, looking at the steam rising from my maple leaf mug. The coffee was black and bitter, just the way I like it.

Murgatroyd parked a large suitcase next to the booth I sat in and slid herself onto the seat opposite.

"That"s a really big suitcase," I said, looking down at the enormous piece of luggage.

"Big shoes, big suitcase. If you fold clown shoes they start to curl at the toes, and they can trip you."

"If I'd known you wanted to be a party clown, I might have handed out different advice," I said, lifting my gaze from the suitcase and looking across at her.

She sat for a moment without responding and then put a hand over her mouth, her eyes bright. Then she dropped her hand and started laughing: joyful, unrestrained, infectious laughter. Before I knew it, I was laughing too. A waitress came out from the kitchen to check on what was happening.

"Oh my God! You thought I want to spend my life as the Happiness Consultant?"

"Well, isn't that what you want to do?"

"Noooo," she said, drawing out the end of the word and throwing it down on the floor. "I want to be a writer!"

"That's a relief. I was worried I'd encouraged you to run off to the circus."

"Clowns are so creepy," she said, shivering theatrically.

"So why do you…?"

"Conference gigs like this pay extremely well."

"Ah," I said. "So how did you get into this particular line of work?"

"It's the family business. My grandmother and dad were both

87

clowns."

"You're very good. I was watching as you worked the crowd yesterday. They were soaking it up."

"Thanks! From what I heard of your speech it sounds like you're pretty good at what you do, too. And that confession at the start. When we spoke you said you'd spent your whole life lining up, following the rules."

"Just because you're good at something doesn"t always mean you love doing it."

"Bullshit! You just enjoy being contrary."

"Is that the type of language you're going to use in your writing?"

"Yes. I'm going to fill my stories with contrarian pains in the butt."

"I was referring to the expletive."

She stood up.

"I have a flight to catch. Thanks. For the advice and the encouragement. It helped."

"There are forces in society that want to take the language hostage, dumb it down and control it," I said, looking up at her. "Writers, the really good ones, help to weaken that hold, make us think in new ways. Have a great life, Murgatroyd. I've got a feeling you'll be a great writer."

"Maybe," she said, smiling down at me then she turned and walked out of the bistro.

IN THE EYES OF A CHILD

Susan Duffield-Lodge

I drop, exhausted, into the chair in the corner of the room to watch my child as she sleeps.

'Five minutes', I whisper to myself. 'Just… five… minutes.' That's how long I intend to spend resting my eyes as they begin to grow heavy.

As I sink into that transitional state between wakefulness and sleep, I'm immediately transported back to the meadow behind the cottage where we'd spent our last normal afternoon together—before all hell broke loose.

With Hallowe'en around the corner, my eight-year-old daughter Prescott has persuaded me to make her a pair of wings for her costume this year, her gappy-toothed smile and, "Pretty please mommy!" clinching the deal.

She so badly wants to be Tinkerbell for trick or treating, and her shout, "Then I can fly up into the sky mommy!" resonates.

It's a beautiful day. I grab my new Nikon 35mm camera, toying with the unfamiliar dials, focusing on Prescott.

I begin spinning in place, capturing her from every angle—pressing the shutter in a race to keep up with each step she takes—the camera locked on auto-focus. Images flash through the view-finder as she dances through the foliage surrounding us.

Transfixed and captivated by her balletic beauty and grace—

her innocent fragility—I ask myself, how did I get so damn lucky? She flutters, floating through the meadow of autumn wildflowers, testing her new iridescent pixie wings. With each twist and twirl the gauzy fabric glows with a vibrant luminescence pierced by the rays of the late afternoon sun.

Drowsily, memories continue to unwind, taking me back in time, in saturated bursts of colour—cinematic kaleidoscopic film-shots playing out on a big screen.

Back to when Prescott asks if it's true, like Granny Murgatroyd told her, that when she was little she'd stood too close to the screen door while it was being painted apple red—and the tiny paint flecks splattered off the brush bristles, travelled through the screen and splashed across her face, and that was why she had so many freckles.

In actuality, Prescott doesn't have an overabundance of them. They lightly sprinkle across the bridge of her nose and trickle down one cheek.

When I answer her 'freckle' question, I tell her that she has just enough freckles to remind me of the constellation, Cassiopeia, and I point it out to her where it sits, up in the Northern sky.

With my mention of Cassiopeia and constellations, she presses me to share everything I know about the night sky, and thus begins Prescott's fascination with the moon and the stars and all things celestial.

Her insatiable appetite to learn all she can about the universe, intensifies her sense of affinity with the galaxies up above.

As the stars sparkle in the night sky, Prescott exclaims with wonder and awe, "They're winking at me 'cause they know that we're kindred spirits!"

I startle and wake to the incessant beeping of an IV pump, the

90

squeak of rubber-soled shoes on linoleum, the murmur of voices.

Prescott is still asleep in the hospital bed as I gently plant a kiss on her pale forehead, noticing, as I lean closer, a fresh coppery splotch on her pillowcase—another nose-bleed—this more profuse than the last. They've been occurring much more frequently.

The morning sun peeks through the blinds as I stand over my daughter's sleeping form, basking in the essence of her; her delicate bone structure, the violet smudged shadows that stain the skin beneath her eyes.

The stark reality suddenly hits home, a punch to the gut, almost bringing me to my knees. Prescott's not going to grow up. She won't have the chance to spread her wings and fly, like she's *so* determined to do, just like Tinkerbell.

I look up to see Dr. Morris, Prescott's oncologist, standing in the doorway. He gestures, mouthing to me, 'Can we talk?'

I begin trembling uncontrollably suspecting the truth he's about to share.

Clearing his throat he imparts the news.

"As you're aware, Prescott's chances of a full recovery were promising when we initially discovered her cancer two years ago. We were confident we'd caught it early.

"We spoke about this sub-group of medulloblastoma and how aggressive in nature it was.

"Unfortunately, Prescott's recent scans show the cancer is no longer in remission. Her tumour has tripled in size.

"This isn't the outcome we were all hoping for. I'm so sorry."

A long pause stretches into an uncomfortable silence and then, "Do you have any questions for me?"

I want to know what to expect as Prescott's condition worsens,

91

now that she's out of remission.

Dr. Morris explains, "Symptoms, much like those Prescott experienced prior to diagnosis are likely to occur now with increasing severity: headaches, seizures, nausea, vertigo, and a deterioration in her visual acuity, which Prescott is already exhibiting, will eventually lead to complete blindness.

"The tumour is causing the intracranial pressure to increase, exacerbating the swelling of Prescott's optic nerves."

His final words are of little consolation. "I'm afraid it's time to have a heart-to-heart with Prescott. Ask her where she'd like to spend her final days."

I don't tell him that asking Prescott that won't be necessary. I know what her answer will be.

There's nowhere Prescott would rather be than at the lake. She loves gathering up the sleeping bags for us to cuddle in out on the dock, where we spend hours admiring the night sky, often falling asleep and awaking at dawn to the melancholy songs of the loons.

By the time Prescott's hospital discharge is processed, her vision has deteriorated further.

She's no longer able to see the stars. The moon has diminished, in her eyes, to a haloed glow in the night sky.

I immediately busy myself making phone-calls to the summer residents on the lake, those I know who won't be closing their cottage up until after the long weekend, eager to discover who might help me in surprising Prescott one last time.

That night we lie out under the canopy of stars, as we've always done, when suddenly, hundreds of sky lanterns begin appearing over the reflective surface of the lake.

The cottagers have, one by one, set them aloft as they'd promised they would. They climb into the inky darkness above, brightly glowing with a warm intensity as they continue their ascent.

I'm unsure if Prescott is able to see them, so I wait patiently, hoping for a sign.

"Mommy?...Mommy?.." I feel her tiny fragile hand tugging gently at my sleeve. "Mommy...I see them! I can see the stars!" and she begins to giggle.

There's nothing in this world that compares to the sound of a child's laughter. It's pure and honest, authentic and guileless, and I marvel each time I hear my child's expression of inordinate joy: the joy she feels in life and in living, at a time when the opposite could just as easily be true.

"Ooooooh...Look at them mommy! Aren't they bea-U-tiful? They're twinkling and winking at me!"

It is at that moment, as Prescott tilts her head back to look up at me, I catch a reflection—a tiny glimpse of the stars in her eyes.

DELILAH

Sherry Cassells

Every once in a while I feel a love story coming on, it's like nourishment.

I don't even remember what *who shot JR* was about that summer, but I remember everything about first time I saw Ted, same summer. He was the friend of Uncle Robert's son whom my parents had met on their previous visit to Coleraine and said *if ever you come to Canada…*

I was driving a blue pickup patchouly laden not quite a flower in my hair but colour, probably, and smoke—I was a glass-blower for a neon company—and he was fresh out of the military, a clean cut lad of undiluted Irish descent and high colour, exquisitely blushed, square. When I hugged him, he smelled of soap, something lavender, he later said he was suddenly overcome with the thought I might lead him astray. My speciality. Perceptive guy.

We raced around the airport like a car chase. I could't find my way out and when I did, I got on the wrong road. It opened up like an invitation, sang like the Salem witches, but I came out of it just in time, did a highly illegal turn, and a couple of hairy minutes later we were on the right road going the right way, Alex Harvey's rendition of Tom Jones' *Delilah* loud from my dangling speakers. I lit a cigarette and smiled over at Ted who was colourless, shaken, but he smiled in a genuine way, and his spreading mouth whispered *Heavens to Murgatroyd* and I just howled

94

That's how he earned his nickname.

My parents were waiting, they had his room, my old one, ready and had "scored" tickets to the Tutankhamun exhibition the following morning and were anxious about the jet lag so they said *bring him straight here we will feed him something light* and they didn't say *and bore him to death* but certainly it was their intention to dance him through the house, a dark tango, his visit a sudden murder ballad.

I saw the light on the night that I passed by her window.

I ended up staying on the couch, I had no work scheduled the next day, Murgatroyd said *can't you come?* and my mother said *there are only three tickets* and I said *I can sneak in* and went with them, I snuck in, such a cinch although the gates were heavily armed and I had the feeling my mother was going to turn me in she disapproved so heartily of me. I was not the daughter she had hoped for, nothing demure about me like the pictures she got from her sister, her two little girls *Prim* and *Grim* I called them, but we had the most wonderful day if you can believe it. In that tomb it was like my parents suddenly approved of me. They laughed instead of tsk-tsking. My mother didn't shake her sad head even once, and on the way out, Murgatroyd opened the crook of his arm for mine and looked at me in a way I'd only seen in movies.

HYSTER/IA

Zilla Jones

"It needs to come out now," says Dr Abrams. "I know we've been trying to preserve your fertility, but-"

I shift position, trying to move my tailbone from the hard leather of the examination table to the comparatively more comfortable paper that crackles beneath my shoulders, wishing I could have my clothes on for this conversation. "I still want to have a child," I venture.

Dr Abrams looks down at my chart. "You are –" he begins to do the math, and I say,

"Forty-seven."

He clears his throat, skims his notes. "Have you and your partner been trying?" He flips a page, skims the next one. "I see you brought a young man to an appointment ten years ago."

"We broke up," I say. An image of Sampson nudges past all the other thoughts to the forefront of my brain. I focus on my memory of his exuberant smile as he hugged me after the launch of Hand 2 Hand, his brand-new mentorship organization for Black business owners. "Murgatroyd, you've put so much love into this, and I promise it will come back to you," he said. Thinking of that moment deprives the next one of oxygen: a one-word text, **Sorry**. Sampson's first communication with me since the night before my admission to hospital for my first myomectomy surgery, a week after I returned home, still aching, still bleeding, my incision a raw yawn below my belly button. The operation had been done to remove my fibroids, but I wished it had also excised my heart. I was thirty-nine then and I had been dating Sampson for four years. It took me several days to realize that that was the last text he would ever send me.

"I don't like the word dumped. You dump garbage, not people. But that's exactly how he treated you. Like garbage," Tonya said when I told her what had happened. She expressed the anger I was afraid to let myself feel, and it infused me with a little steel, a little spit, just enough not to break.

I fix my eyes on the diagram on the wall; the stages of development of a fetus. *Not a fetus,* I think, *a baby.* I shake my head, hearing the paper wrinkle and tear behind my ponytail.

"Well, let's take another look, shall we?" I wince as Dr Abrams picks up the plastic wand. I am a virgin. I don't even use tampons. This wand – the child-size model - is the only thing that has ever gone inside me.

"Just relax," coaches Dr Abrams, which only makes me tense up more. He presses on my abdomen. "Your stomach will get smaller after we take these things out," he comments, all but patting me on the head as he says it. It's true: my mid-section is so swollen, I look like I am expecting, but rather than being pregnant with hope and elation, I am the future mother of emptiness and despair.

Dr Abrams points to the screen and I see the black ultrasound triangle, so familiar from countless triumphant posts on Facebook, but instead of housing a tangle of limbs, mine is filled with vibrating invaders. "You see how big they are?" says Dr Abrams. "Your fibroids are growing into the uterine cavity. That's why the bleeding is so heavy. If we don't do the hysterectomy, the blood loss will become more severe from now until menopause. Your quality of life will be affected."

It is already affected. Every month, I soak through super-sized pads, my clothing and my sheets, until my legs give way under me like a folding stool. I fainted in the office twice last month.

"So everything looks good to go ahead with the operation next Monday," Dr Abrams decides for me.

I understand. My uterus has not served its intended purpose. Use it or lose it. The days and the weeks have packed together, a pile of rock and debris growing higher and higher against the calendar, and now there is no more time.

I still have time, I correct myself on the drive home. *The only way I can keep going is to stay positive.* This is what my mother always says to do. This is why I surround myself with inspiring meditations and Biblical quotes, or take smiling selfies and post them on Instagram, then tell everyone else how beautiful their own pictures are, in the hope that they will return the compliment. Gone are the days when I stood crying in front of my mirror at the sight of my broad-shouldered, wide-hipped frame, my dark skin and kinky-rooted hair. After work, I turn up my speakers and dance to uplifting music. Dance is something I had always hoped to share with my children some day.

I turn on the radio at the top of the hour to hear the news. So much of it is negative: plane crashes, civil war, and some racist remarks by an elected official. I am about to switch over to the music stored in my phone when the announcer says, *The Royal Canadian Air Force Snowbirds are embarking on a cross-country tour, and they fly over Winnipeg next week.*

I feel my body relaxing into the seat. I have been so preoccupied with my surgery that I had temporarily forgotten about my favorite event of the year. Some big, loud planes are exactly what I need. Their grinding, vibrating engines, the combination of power and grace as they dip and dive above the rooftops in their signature Canada goose formation, are guaranteed to make me feel better. Perhaps I can watch the planes with my nephew,

Jackson. The thought of the Snowbirds has restored to me the hope that Dr Abrams stole from me. Women get pregnant at forty-seven; it's not impossible.

"You have to be married before you let a man touch you, Murgatroyd," my mother counseled when I got my first period. I developed breasts before any other girl in my class, but my mother pretended obliviousness to my changing body and continued to send me bra-less to school in smocked flowered dresses that strained over my chest. Along with my strange name, Murgatroyd, a throwback to my mother's English grandfather, it was another reason for the kids to tease me. "The Bible says a woman is to only be known by one man, for life," my mother warned. *Be known* was the only way she ever spoke of sex.

But why? I ask myself now. I know from my own studies that the Bible doesn't say what my mother says it does. It counsels in favor of chastity and against sexual immorality, but it doesn't speak to loving relationships between two adults. I allow myself to think the unthinkable: what if I meet someone right away, and we have sex right away, and against all odds, I get pregnant? Wouldn't the sin be worth the reward? Wouldn't that be better than lifelong celibacy and eternal childlessness? But I can't completely blame my mother for my current situation: my own self-imposed dating criteria played a part. This is what my sister-in-law Delaine has said time and time again. The first time was right before I met Sampson.

"Maybe you should consider dating other guys, not just Black ones," she suggested. I gaped at her, the very idea heretical. On a prior occasion when Delaine had had too many cocktails, she had confessed that she had only married my brother Corey so that they could have children. This time, Delaine was pregnant with Jackson and assuredly not drunk, her stomach straining against her empire waist top and maternity jeans.

"I'm just not attracted to other guys," I said. "I want to be with someone who looks like me and shares my experiences, my culture." It is what my mother has always told me – don't bother with white men, stick with your own.

"Sure, Murg," Delaine said, "but at some point, if you want kids, you just gotta settle." She, who had not had to settle, at least not in terms of race, gave her baby bump a smug pat. It was my desire to prove her wrong that spurred my first exploration of the dating site where I met Sampson.

We were both thirty-five then. It seems young to me now, but back then, thirty-five was an age when the river you were swimming in started rushing, carrying you over rapids, smashing you into your future.

Tonya has been my best friend since kindergarten, the only other Black girl in the class. After she takes my profile picture for Plenty of Fish, following a bout of fussing with lipstick and lighting, we turn our attention to the qualities I am seeking in a partner. When Tonya gets to 'Preferred race', her cocked finger hovers over the button, curved like a question mark.

"Black, of course," I say. "But the last time I put that, I got a ton of guys harassing me, saying I was a reverse racist."

"Put that you want someone who's been to the Caribbean, likes soca music and is a Christian," Tonya advises. "Not too many white guys fit that bill, and then you don't have to write 'Black guys only' and take peoples' shit."

I watch her type. My name, *Murgatroyd*, blares from the screen. I wonder how many guys will think it's a weird name, not feminine enough, should be a last name.

Once my profile is submitted, Tonya says, "Girl! There's this new DJ, here in Winnipeg, who's *fire*. He does these *lit* online dance parties." Tonya has fallen into the habit of talking like her sixteen-year-old daughter, Onyika. When Tonya turned thirty, she decided it was time to have a baby, and she deliberately got pregnant by a man she never intended to marry. I didn't do a very good job of hiding my shock, but Tonya is having the last laugh now as the mother of a feisty sixteen-year-old daughter. Onyika used to sleep over at my place every weekend when she was little and Tonya was working nights, so Tonya still refers to me as Onyika's second mother.

Tonya loads DJ Smalls' Facebook page onto her phone and holds it out to me. The camera loves him, and his mahogany skin, full lips and treacly eyes make my heart swing forward in my chest.

"Wow," I say, "what a beautiful man." My body is tingling, and I imagine my mother saying, *Lust is a sin, Murgatroyd.* I push her voice away, wanting privacy inside my own head.

"Isn't he?" Tonya exclaims. "I'd have his babies." She bites her lip. "Sorry, Murg."

"It's OK." Despite the many times I have told her about my longing for a baby, it irritates me that Tonya pities me. I should pity her. Life as a single mother has not been easy for Tonya. In fact, life for any mother can be a challenge. I work in Human Resources, and over the years, my office has hosted a parade of women crying about how they need accommodations for sick kids or lack of childcare. I may not have a child, but I have other roads to happiness; church, and the dance classes I teach, and my own dancing. And planes. Mechanical birds, a marvel of human imagination that swoop through the space above us, carrying our desires from place to place; planes bring me joy.

The next day, I hear on the news that Winnipeg police have shot a Black man, his cell phone mistaken for a gun, and a familiar well of pain opens up in my stomach. I need something positive to

101

think about, and I remember that I haven't asked Delaine about watching the Snowbirds with Jackson. He can come up to the roof of my condo and see everything up close. They fly over next Saturday, and my surgery is next Monday. Watching the Snowbirds will be the last happy thing I do before I go to the hospital.

Jackson answers Delaine's phone and I wonder when he started doing that. "Hi Aunt Murgatroyd!" he yells. He sounds younger than his eleven years. Delaine tends to treat Jackson like a baby, because he's her only child. She had originally wanted more children, but after her pregnancy with Jackson, marked by pre-gestational diabetes, pre-eclampsia and an emergency C-section, she said,

"I'm done. My body wasn't made for this. I'm never doing this again."

"Maybe you'll change your mind later," I suggested, but Delaine's mouth turned downwards in a grimace.

"No way. I'm too old anyway," she said, her words great furrows scraped across my heart by a careless plow.

Delaine takes the phone from Jackson, and I make my suggestion about the Snowbirds.

"Oh," she says. "I don't know if we'll have time for that. Jackson has online tutoring every Saturday now. He's really behind in math." She sighs. "And I don't know if you heard, but the cops killed another Black guy. Black Lives Matter is planning a protest, and I'm supposed to be helping."

I would rather not talk about that. There is enough sorrow in my heart. Having loved one Black man, I grieve for all of them. I don't protest, I mourn. "Anyway, I don't really agree with the air show," Delaine says. "Jet fuel is so bad for the environment."

Rather than enter the debate, I say, "Also, my surgery's a go." I want someone to stop me from giving up my womanhood, tell me that my dream of conception isn't dead.

"Oh, yeah," Delaine says. I can tell I am on speaker phone by the echo. I hear the clink of cutlery.

"I'm not sure if I'm going to get it done," I say, trying to sound casual.

"Why not?" asks Delaine. "I wish someone would take *my* uterus out. It's not like I need it any more and it's a real pain in the ass, literally. My PMS was so effing bad yesterday."

I know she has moderated her language only because Jackson is still there, and sure enough, he shouts, "Mom, I'm done. Can I play X-box now?"

Delaine has stripped my wounds open again with her reminder that, like most of the women I know from work, the gym and church, she has fulfilled her biological destiny and I have not. But I must remain positive, and Delaine's hormonal rages are not a topic I wish to discuss.

"Just letting you know!" I say in the perkiest voice I can muster. "Gotta go. God bless."

I text Tonya and ask her if she wants to come over and watch the Snowbirds with me. I don't want to be alone the day before a scalpel cuts into me and removes the deepest cry of my heart from its dwelling place.

I spend the day speaking to the staff of the company I work for, doing my weekly well-being check ins. Many of the mothers are overwhelmed by their attempts to balance their work and home lives. A streak of gratitude flashes through me as I recognize the time and space with which I am blessed. The luxury of worrying only for and about myself.

I teleconference with the rest of the management team, and then I go to the den I have converted into a studio and dance to my playlist of "Uplifting tunes." When I am finished, I see that I have missed a call from my mother. I call her back right away.

"Murgatroyd!" she shouts, panting with the effort of hurrying to the phone. "Miz Johnson from the church died!" She says this as if the urgency and tragedy of it should be obvious to me. I barely knew Miz Johnson, and she was well into her nineties. "The funeral's on Monday. Pastor said he'd love it if you did one of the readings."

Monday is the day of my surgery. *Thank you, Lord,* I say to myself. *You do answer prayer. This could be my deliverance.*

My mother has the same realization. She says, "Oh, no, wait, isn't that when you have your operation?"

"Maybe I can postpone it."

"Didn't the doctor say it needs to come out now?"

"Yes, but Mom, I'm not sure if I even want to get the operation."

"Murgatroyd, everyone has to bear their cross," my mother says, "and this is yours. I would have loved you to marry and have children, but look at what else you've done with your life. A masters degree, all those awards. Marriage is a calling from God, and not everyone is called. There are obligations to others as well."

Her words tear into my chest with the speed and destruction of a bullet. Heedlessly, she continues, "You must count your blessings. You must, what do they say, practice gratitude."

She kept me single and inviolate. She has ensured that there is no competition for her affection, her needs. And I am supposed to be grateful.

As those thoughts roar through me, I rock forward with their force. I have never thought of my mother as controlling. I have always assumed she had my best interests at heart.

I turn from the pain and go to DJ Smalls' Instagram account. Tonight he will broadcast another online dance party. He says that as we dance along at home, we become connected to the kitchens and basements of all the other dancers. Several women have commented,

Does it have to be at night? I have to put the kids to bed and the music will wake them up.

Are the lyrics kid-friendly, LOL?

I would do it, but we're taking the kids to Six Flags that day and we'll be exhausted.

I have no such limitations, and my body sparks with anticipation of the dancing to come.

I take a spinach and chicken pizza from my freezer. I bought it for Jackson the last time I babysat, but when I showed him the box, he frowned. "What's that green stuff?" he asked. I put the pizza back and made Kraft dinner.

"KD?" Delaine said when she picked him up. "That's all he eats. I was hoping you'd get him to try something else." I explained about the pizza, and she said, "Jackson doesn't eat spinach, or broccoli. I thought you knew. It's a nightmare feeding him."

I eat the pizza in front of the TV, my feet up on the couch. After the first slice, I feel the urge to have wine. I know the Bible says drunkenness is wrong, and my mother would be horrified to see me consuming any amount of alcohol, but one glass, just one, has a way of adding a little glow, so that pizza in front of the TV becomes a privilege instead of a prison.

The calmness of DJ Smalls' voice makes me feel like I have slipped into a warm bath. The nuggets of wisdom he imparts in between songs seem to be those of someone much older than his actual age, which I calculate to be somewhere in his late twenties. My spirits are buoyed by the knowledge that he is out there in my neighborhood, that I could bump into him in the grocery store at any time, that there is the possibility I will someday know how he smells and how his young body feels, if only for an instant. *Lust is a sin,* I remind myself, even as I yearn for another pixelated glimpse of him.

The next morning, there are three alerts on my phone. The hospital, confirming that my surgery will go ahead on Monday. A news alert that Winnipeg police have shot another unarmed Black man. And a missed call from Delaine.

My mind is a ball of yarn, spooling and unspooling in a tangle of neurons and synapses, as I press Delaine's icon.

"Murgatroyd? How are things?" Delaine is breathless, her voice scratchy.

"Is this a bad time?"

"Oh," she says, trying to sound casual, but I recognize the note of stress in her voice. "Jackson's behind in his homework, and we're trying to get his math worksheet done before school."

On the other end of the call, I hear Jackson yelling in the background, "I hate math! Math is trash!"

"Be quiet and eat your breakfast if you're not going to finish the questions!" Delaine yells, then, "Sorry, Murgatroyd, you were saying?"

"You called me," I say.

"Oh, did I? I must have pocket-dialed you. Sorry."

"The Snowbirds are here on Monday," I remind her. Even though I know she has already decided.

"Yeah," she says. "I dunno. It's so militaristic and I'm trying to get Jackson away from toxic masculinity."

Jackson yells, "I hate everything."

Her voice wavers as she says, "I'll talk to you later. After Jackson gets on the school bus, I'm going to try to set up an office. I'm so sick of trying to get work done in the kitchen - it's just nuts. We don't have any extra rooms so I'm going to have to do it in the hallway, you know, by the bathroom upstairs?"

My suite has an extra bedroom, and I've left it mostly empty in the hopes that someday it might become a nursery. I hung pictures of planes on the wall that I thought a baby might enjoy, but when I look at them, they give me comfort too. The spare bedroom would make a lovely office, with a view of the river. I open the door and step into the circles of sunlight on the carpet, seeing promise in the emptiness for the first time.

On Saturday morning, I reflect on the daily Bible verse my pastor emailed to the congregation yesterday. An oldie but a goodie: *I can do anything through God who strengthens me.* But that's not true, I think. If I can do anything, why can't I get married? Quicker than I can finish that thought, the next one slides in behind it: perhaps God is strengthening me to do something else. As my mother says, not everyone is called to marriage. My mother has misled me about a lot of things, but she was right about that.

I look across the roof at Tonya, sprawled on my lounger, and I wonder if Jackson is, after all, watching the skies too. Delaine swore he was never going to go trick o' treating, but every year, he's the kid with the most elaborate costume and biggest pail of candy on the block.

The familiar hole opens up inside me, the wind howling through. I mothered Tonya's daughter and I mother Jackson, but what I wouldn't have give to have a fetus – not a fetus, *a baby* - flipping around my womb instead of this heavy treachery of muscle and tissue pulsing within me. My phone rings and I snatch it from the table, grateful for the distraction.

"Aunt Murgatroyd!" yells Jackson. "They're flying over us right now!" A roar buzzes through the phone, distorting his words. "The planes! They're here!" he exults.

"Wow!" I yell back at Jackson. "Isn't it incredible, Jax?"

Delaine's voice chimes in. "The teacher postponed the

deadline for the worksheet so the kids could watch the damn planes." She sounds tired. "I think they're headed in your direction now."

Sure enough, a distant hum becomes a growl and whirls into a groaning, grinding weight of vibrations as the planes slice through the air above. One of them breaks away and traces a heart in pink smoke right above my building. I watch it loop the loop and rejoin the others. Even a piece of machinery has a family, belongs somewhere.

The tears bubble up, throbbing like the engines of the jets. I could have obeyed my body's signals and had sex with Sampson, even without marriage. Maybe then he wouldn't have left me. Maybe then I would have a child now even if he did leave. My mother would have said it was wrong, but what was wrong was hewing so closely to her beliefs, her voice, that my desires never sang for themselves.

The sun casts a haze to the east, its feeble rays barely warming the earth, as the planes hang suspended above its golden wash. I can still cancel the operation. I can call the hospital and give some excuse, say I'm not feeling well, then go online and meet someone, anyone, any color. Defy every teaching with which I was raised, and have sex again and again and again until somehow my mind wills my body into creating a baby and my old womb creaks to life and bears fruit. I can do now what I should have done ten years ago. Through the film of my tears, I watch the planes flock together and speed into the glinting embrace of the sun.

"Hey," Tonya says. "It's going to be OK, Murg." She walks toward me with her arms outstretched, but before she can give me a hug, my phone buzzes. I pick it up and read a text from Delaine. **Call Jax after they fly over.** I swipe my arm over my eyes and dial.

"Aunt Murgatroyd!" Jackson shouts. "Did they draw a heart?"

"They did, pumpkin," I manage. Tonya goes back to her lounger and looks down at her own phone.

"That's my heart to you," Jackson says. "Mom says that you're going to the hospital and you need some extra love."

I try to stifle my sobs. "Th-thanks, sweetheart."

I hear Delaine's voice in the background, but can't make out the words.

"I gotta go," Jackson says.

I am still staring at the sky where the pink smoke drifts, the shape of the heart gradually collapsing into an oval, when I see something that is not supposed to happen. A white flash, and then black smoke. A ball of fire. A flaming figure dangling from a parachute, floating down past the roofs a block or two away. The other planes turning back, converging on the conflagration in the great blue void where seconds ago, a metal craft seemed invincible. Where a sign of love and hope has burned into terror. I already know what the tributes to the pilot will say. *They died doing what they loved to do. They soared in a way most of us never get to do. From the greatest heights we plunge to the depths of sorrow.*

"Oh my God," says Tonya.

Oh my God, protect them, I plead, even though I know that there are some things God cannot, or will not, do. Tonya taps the screen of her phone. "It's on Twitter already," she reports. "Everybody's posting what happened. The wreckage is on some guy's lawn. There's a body."

I know my thoughts should be with the downed pilot, but instead, I am thinking of how Jackson said that heart was for me. A puff of smoke, so easily made, so easily broken, so easily forgotten, and yet it was etched, if even for only a moment, on the greatest canvas the earth will ever know. It is enough. It will never be enough, and yet it is.

I look across the yard at Tonya, still engrossed in her phone. "It's too late, isn't it?" I ask. I am not speaking of the life of the pilot or the crash we just witnessed.

"Too late for kids," she says. "Not too late for pretty much anything else. Well, maybe to become an Olympic gymnast." She laughs a short, high bark.

I could go to Tonya and let her give me a hug, cry on her shoulder, and then call the hospital and tell them I can't make my appointment. But once again, the buzz of my phone saves me. It is an alert from Plenty of Fish and it seems Tonya was wrong, because a very blond, dreadlocked man has been to St. Lucia where he fell in love with soca, and loves to cook roti and doubles and praise God, and we have matched. He wants to meet for coffee and a walk next weekend. He has a nice smile. **Murgatroyd,** he has written. **That's a great name. So unique.** My finger readies itself to delete his message, and the thought comes, *Why not, Murgatroyd?*

I start to type, **I'd like to get together soon but**

"I should get the surgery, shouldn't I?" I ask Tonya, even as I write, **I'm having a medical procedure done, so maybe we can meet up when I'm recovered.**

"You know what you should do right now?" says Tonya, swinging her long legs over the edge of the lounger. "You should dance with me. I just got an alert from DJ Smalls – there's another dance party about to go live. The theme is 'Dancing Against Police Brutality.' Right on, hey?" She raises a clenched fist.

Dance is one of the many things I had hoped to share with my children someday. But dance is for everyone, not just for mothers. Dance is for the last day before they take your uterus, and for the first day you'll get out of bed afterward. It is for the moments following a fatal plane crash. When someone has given their life to lift your spirits, you should let them stay lifted. And dance is for the days after police bullets fell two Black men, just to show that even if they are gone, you are still here. Their lives mattered because yours still does. The body is fragile and does not always do what we wish it would, does not always survive all that we ask of it. Dance is how our flesh and bones realize that they have more than one destiny, and we should embrace the one in which we find ourselves.

"Should we, though?" I ask, even as my limbs itch to loosen in the abandon of bass, keyboards and a honeyed voice putting into words all my feelings of love, loss and loneliness. "I mean, we just saw-"

Tonya snaps her fingers. "We don't know that pilot," she says. "It's not gonna change anything if we sit around here and mope." *This is positivity*, I think. *This is optimism.*

"Go get your speakers and we'll have us a party!" Tonya is already on her feet, her hips swaying back and forth.

I join in, waving my arms in the air and shimmying from side to side. I rejoice in the delicious collision of rhythms stitched together by DJ Smalls.

Tonya's anger on my behalf gave me courage when I needed it, but her smile hands me the future. I shout over the music, "Girl, this man is so gorgeous. I need to have his babies."

"Me, too," she agrees.

I rotate my hips, dip my shoulders, and feel the rhythm slide down my spine all the way to my pelvis.

Aunt Ida's Apple Tree

Shawn L. Bird

"I wouldn't marry you if the flames of hell were devouring Aunt Ida's apple tree, and copulation could save the human race! Do you hear me, Billy Killswell? For the four hundredth time, the answer is no!"

I had meant it, too. I'd meant it the three hundred and ninety nine times previously, and the seventy-eight times after. So what was I doing here in this damn white dress standing beside him?

Four hundred seventy nine is a charm, apparently.

Billy grinned over at me.

I snarled back.

His grin widened.

If I only I'd held out for four hundred and eighty. Four-eighty is definitely a number full of secure denial.

Damn Billy Killswell. Damn him from now 'til eternity.

"I told you I'd get you here, didn't I?" Billy whispered.

"To hell with you, Billy." I muttered back.

Pastor Griffith gave a little start, and looked down his bi-focals at me. I scowled as he cleared his throat and motioned the congregation to sit down. The entire congregation consisted of half-blind Brody Turner and my cousin Lula, who were the designated witnesses to this farce.

"Dearly beloved…" Griff intoned solemnly.

"Stop!" bellowed a voice from the back, and all nine eyes in the church turned to stare at the door. "Everyone come! There's a fire at Ida's!"

Billy looked at me suspiciously.

"How could I have anything to do with it? I've been right here, haven't I?" I declared in response to the silent accusation on his face.

"Keep going," Billy said to Griff.

Brody and Lula were already out the door.

Griff shook his head. "Sorry. No witnesses. No wedding."

I grinned and Billy glared at me. "They'll sign afterwards." He grabbed my wrists. The daisies wobbled and their slightly rotten scent wafted between us.

Griff was pulling off his stole and tucking his Bible on its shelf behind the podium.

A strange scream came from outside.

Griff started sprinting down the aisle, calling over his shoulder, "Sorry, Billy! It'll have to be another time."

I turned, and Billy grabbed my shoulder. "Where do you think you're going?"

"Fighting a fire?" I tried to shake him off, but he was holding me firmly.

"We're doing this, Murg."

"Not at the moment, we're not. Let go, Billy." Shouts and crashing came through the door and the distant sound of the volunteer fire brigade on their way. "They need you." With any luck I'd be able to sneak off while he was busy.

Smoke was billowing up, from dancing golden flames, but it wasn't the house. It was Ida's apple tree, nestled next to the barn. Already sparks were glowing on the barn roof. The horses were squealing, as Lula and Brody were running in to open the stalls. "Watch your dress, Lula!"

Pauly pulled up in the fire truck, "Billy! Help me with the

hoses!"

Billy scowled at me. "Don't you dare go anywhere."

I blinked at him innocently and received a well-deserved look with skeptically raised eyebrows.

After three years of haunting me at the diner and proposals nearly twice a week, the boy knew me well.

"Psst!"

I looked around.

"In the church!" came a frantic whisper.

I backed up slowly, but stayed in the open door way, to glare at Billy who checked for me as he pulled a hose toward the barn.

"Ida? Is that you?" I whispered out the side of my mouth.

"Who else would dare set fire to my tree?"

I chuckled at that, and checking that Billy wasn't watching, slipped inside. Aunt Ida engulfed me in a bone crushing hug. For someone who wasn't much over four feet tall, she was remarkably strong. I guess years of breaking horses and hauling hay bales will do that to a person.

She studied me up and down. "Nice dress."

I scoffed. "Thrift store. I think it was Marian Hemsley's." Marian had died in the spring. Her sons had emptied her house into the thrift store.

Ida squinted thoughtfully. "Oh, yes. That makes sense. Lovely wedding, that one. Marian was a happy bride."

"She wasn't a very happy wife though, was she?"

A shout went up outside and Ida smirked, ignoring my comment. "Come with me, Murgatroyd."

The fire truck started up.

"What's going on?" I said, glancing to the door.

"That'll be the far hay field igniting. I used your Uncle Davey's delayed fuse technique. Remember how he'd set smoke bombs to go off in the boy's can at the community dances?"

114

"I've head the stories. Why are you setting fires?"

Ignoring me, she opened the door to the custodian cupboard, reached into the back, and pulled the whole cupboard out the door jam. It was a cement stairwell.

I stared at her.

"In you go, sweetheart. We'll talk where we won't be interrupted. It won't take them long to deal with that field."

She hit a light switch and pulled the shelf unit behind us. I heard the cupboard door close automatically behind it.

At the bottom of the stairs was another door. She shut off the stair light, and we stepped into what appeared to be a well-appointed apartment as the solid metal door thudded closed behind us. A little kitchen occupied one corner, a fold down bed had another one, and a TV sat on a shelf with a good stock of DVDs. There was a computer at a desk.

"What is this place?"

"Originally, it was a bomb shelter, back in the sixties when the Russians had their missiles aimed at Refinery Row in Edmonton. Davey got a little paranoid after all those drills they had us do, hiding under our desks and all. Then he got all worried about the *Wizard of Oz* and keeping me safe from tornadoes. Just before he died it was all about the Millennium Bug." She shrugged. "I've fixed it up a bit over the years. It's not just a hole in the ground, either. There is a tunnel leading to the well shed, and another one from the house." She indicated what looked like cupboard doors, one behind the sofa, the other near the stairs.

"Why?"

She shrugged. "It's always good to have a safe place to escape to. When Davey built the chapel on the property, he figured it was a place of double sanctuary. You know, as if God wouldn't let tornadoes or bombs touch a church." She shook her head in fond amusement. "Davey was a paranoid fool, but he was devoted to my safety. Luckily, he was paranoid enough about it not to tell a soul about this place. I never have either, so no one will be able to find you. There's even internet, and you can watch outside through the security cameras, as well." She switched on the computer.

"Aunt Ida. This is crazy."

"Not as crazy as you marrying that boy in Marian Hemsley's old dress. No matter how nice you look in it," she added.

"I'm glad you feel that way. Everyone else seems to think I'm supposed to reward his years of obsession."

The computer screen was showing the yard of the ranch. People were milling around frantically. Pauly was winding up the fire hose. Lula was staring blankly toward the apple tree. Brody was covered in soot and rubbing his eye. Billy was shouting and gesticulating wildly.

I smiled.

Ida watched the screen. "There's a fine line between devotion and obsession."

"Tell me about it."

She chuckled. "It seemed to me you should be clear in your mind. How many hundred times did you refuse that boy?" She glanced at me.

I inhaled deeply and didn't bother to give her the gritty details.

"I'm more interested in the one time you said 'yes,' though." She watched me carefully. "How did Billy Killswell get you to agree?"

I took the kettle off the stove and began filling it with water. I set it back on the stove and said, "Tell me about Marian Hemsley's wedding."

Ida watched me and went to sit on the sofa.

Neither of us spoke while the kettle boiled. I dropped a bag into the teapot. "Please?"

I handed her a mug and she cupped it, watching me. "*You* are not Marian Killswell Helmsley."

"I know," but I shuddered anyway.

"Billy is not Noel Helmsley, either."

I looked away. I wasn't convinced of that.

She sighed, staring into the past. "Marian adored Noel Helmsley. She scribbled his name over all her books in school. She designed that dress in art class, and it was her final project in sewing class. By all accounts, Noel adored her as well. Whenever he was in town, he would show up where she was, joking and preening. He took her driving in that red Mustang of his." She glanced up at me, "Her daddy hated that car. He didn't trust anyone who didn't drive a truck. He hated Noel, too. He always said there was something about him that was a greasy as an oil slick."

"Her daddy was a wise man."

"As it turns out, yes. Of course, at the time, we all thought he was being over-protective. Marian's mom liked Noel, though, and she carried the day. Marian had her dream wedding."

She sipped her tea and looked over at me. "Do I need to go on?"

"He already had a wife."

"He did. One in Red Deer and one in Calgary. And another one somewhere up north. Though I suspect that one came after Marian."

"How long before Marian knew?"

"Oh, something like twenty years, I guess. She was a naïve little thing. He travelled, working on the rigs. At least that's what he said."

"And then he killed her."

"What?" She looked up at me with wide eyes. "Where on Earth did you hear that?"

"I thought it was common knowledge."

"Oh, good grief. It was Lula, wasn't it? That girl gossips like words are air." She gave an exasperated sigh and said firmly, "No. Marian wasn't murdered. She had cancer. I was with her when Dr. Thomas gave her the diagnosis."

"Lula said there was blood all over the place."

"Yes. She bled to death, but from the cancer."

"But..."

"Hon, I should have been with her, and I wasn't. I told her I'd be there until the end, and I failed her. I feel damn guilty about it, and I'd appreciate if you don't ask for details. It was cancer. Not Noel."

"He didn't love her."

"Of course, he did!"

I gaped at her.

"He was a polygamist. That just meant he married other people, too. I figured he loved her and didn't want to hurt her." She glanced at my face and added, "I'm not saying he wasn't a deluded ass, but he *did* love her. When we found her, he wept like a baby. I'm sure he loved each of the others as well."

"The two of you found her together?"

She blushed with a curt, "We did."

I grunted.

"Why did you say 'yes.'?" she asked again.

"It was a moment of weakness." I looked at the computer screen again, where Billy was standing off by his car, holding my bouquet of stinky wilting daisies.

"A moment of weakness or a moment of acknowledgment?" She raised her eyebrows at my expression. "Come on. We'd all have been blinder than Brody not to see what you two feel about each other. From that first day, the attraction between you was practically sheet lightning. People leave the diner with so much static electricity that they shock themselves opening their car doors."

I rolled my eyes.

"Three years we've watched. Billy told me about the long heart to heart talks and all the things you have in common. Everyone in town could see it all plainly enough. The only mystery was why you kept saying 'no.' Now I'm wondering whether the more important question is why you said 'yes' that one time."

On the screen Billy was looking down the road with an anguished expression. Damn Billy Killswell. So cute. So charming. So damned insistent. Would I ever love anyone like I loved him?

"Ida. Did you know my mom?" I asked suddenly.

"I don't think so. When was she in town?"

"Never. It's just..." I stopped, thinking. "Did you ever wonder why I came here?"

She grinned. "It was talk all over town when you took the job at the diner and the room over it. I just figured you were here to escape something."

I nodded. "My mom had found out my father was a bigamist."

She tilted her head warily. "Oh?"

"So, I thought I'd see what his other wife was like."

She was fast. Her eyes grew wide. "Oh, God."

"I'm sure there's a law about marrying someone you're related to."

"Oh good glorious God in heaven, you can't be serious?"

I nodded breathing heavily. "I can't marry Billy Killswell no matter what I feel about him. It's sick. He's like my half-brother or something. It's gross." I shuddered again.

"He's not your half-brother. Billy's father is Marian's brother Nathan. Billy'd be your cousin."

"That's still gross."

119

"Except he's not. I mean, not by blood. Nathan was adopted."

"What?" My heart dropped.

"Well, it's not common knowledge," she smirked at me. "Let's see. Back in '58 Suzie Turner got pregnant by Rich Clarke from over by Leduc." She nodded conspiratorially, "He was married, too, the ass. But Suzie never had any judgment. Her mother was Marian's best friend. Suzie died and Nathan went to live with the Killswells. Back then they kept adoptions secret, but Marian told me."

"So, I'm *not* related to Billy?" I looked back at the computer screen at Billy's melancholy face, buried in the daisies.

"Not by blood, no."

"Would you like to take the tunnel into the house?" Ida asked, setting down her teacup. "We'll tell them we've been there all along, shall we?"

"Yes." I said, setting my own cup in the sink. "Sorry about your apple tree."

She giggled. "Well. It's better to marry than to burn, St. Paul says. That tree was a sacrifice for truth. Now you know."

"Yes." I smiled at her. "Now I know."

A NEW EARTH
Finnian Burnett

"First class to the left," Murgatroyd says automatically, bored already as she takes passes and pushes first-class passengers along. "Don't hold up the line." Many of them, the first-class ones, push their passes at her without sparing her a glance.

"Economy to the right," she says, waving a smiling family unit to the lift for the lower decks. No windows below, no decorations, either. She wonders for a moment how long their excited anticipation will last in the dimly lit halls below. Still.

"Enjoy your trip," she calls after them.

They wave back at her, still smiling as the lift doors close. Their faces stay with her, many of them. Hopeful, anxious. Brave people looking to escape the ravages of their home planet. She wants to hug all the lower decks passengers, to tell them the journey will be bad, but the reward will be worth it.

Murgatroyd has been working the Earth emigration ships for ten years and they've barely made a dent in the population. Still, at least the system is fairer than she'd expected when she had first been hired by the company. Rich and poor alike can book passage, and no one in the lower decks has to pay for their travel. Though, of course, the rich get better accommodations.

It's a six-month journey and people who can afford to pay for the luxury of room, spread out over the upper decks, with holographic picture windows and double-sized cabins and separate storage units into which they've paid extra to cram their paintings and electronics and bags of gold.

Murgatroyd sighs and accepts another bunch of pass-holders. This time, it's a group of scientists, climate change activists who'd done their best in the last few years to save the planet before deciding to leave for the new one. She waves them down to the lower decks. No room for middle-class on immigration ships—just long rows of economy bunks, each with a trunk bedside for the one piece of carryon luggage each passenger is permitted to bring.

The scientists smile and chat with Murgatroyd while waiting for the lift. She offers to meet them later in the lower decks mess hall. *Bound to be a great conversation at that table.*

During a break in the line, Murgatroyd watches a crane lift a pallet of belongings onto the upper decks. She grins. A couch, for Christ's sake. Someone is bringing a couch into space? She's still laughing when a family approaches and the youngest, a child of maybe four, hands her the passes with trembling hands.

"Will we see aliens on the ship?" he asks her, wonder in his voice.

Murgatroyd crouches in front of him, smiling. "We are the aliens now," she says. "But," she continues, patting him on the head, "when we round the argon nebula, I'll make sure to point out the planet where the Torrexcians live. They're our new friends."

The child grins and rushes toward the lift with his family. Lower decks, of course. It would be an uncomfortable six months, but the reward of their new home at the end of the journey would make it worthwhile.

Two men in three-piece suits clomp up the ramp, cookie-cutter wives a few steps behind. "I must protest that there isn't a separate entrance for first class," one of them says as soon as he reaches Murgatroyd's station. He stares back at the line, a disdainful sneer curling his lip. "I've been standing in line with *these people* for hours."

These people. Murgatroyd looks out over the hundreds of people still in line—families, workers, teachers, librarians. Some people carry nothing but a beloved book or stuffed animal. Most are exhausted and hungry by the time they make it to the ship, but everyone gets a meal once aboard and no one will starve on New Earth.

One of the wives clutches a tiny dog. Murgatroyd reaches for it.

"All pets go to the lower decks," she says. "We'll take good care of them there."

"Boo-boo stays with me," the wife says, pouting, and though Murgatroyd's orders were to give the wealthy whatever they asked for, on this subject, she puts her foot down. "All pets go to lower decks. We don't have the capacity to care for them on the upper decks."

The woman opens her mouth to protest, but the ship's security is there. The woman looks into the stern face of the uniformed guards and thrusts her pet toward Murgatroyd. "You better take care of her," she says, and turns away. Murgatroyd hands the little dog over to one of the guards, resisting the urge to kiss its fuzzy head. "Take it down to the kennels."

Most passengers don't raise a fuss over giving up their pets for the duration, but some do. Animals need special considerations to be safe in space and the staff can't do that if the pets are scattered throughout private cabins. Besides, Murgatroyd thinks, giving the woman her most ingratiating company smile. Pets have a much better time in the lower decks, even separated from their owners. Murgatroyd herself often visits the pet area to make sure all the animals are treated right. In her previous life, she'd worked at a shelter, and she still loves dogs and cats more than most people. Murgatroyd doesn't bother to reassure the woman, but the dog will be well cared for, fed, and watered. Like the people on the lower decks, the dogs won't have much space, but they'll be tended and treated well, and they'll be happy to run free in the wild grasses of New Earth at the end of the journey.

The two men, oil executives, according to their passes, take their wives' arms and head for the upper deck lift. She watches the lift door close behind them. The hugely inflated cost to make the voyage on the upper deck is more than most people make in their lifetimes. The money funds climate change and world hunger programs on old Earth, but it also covers the energy needed for the round-trip immigration. On New Earth, they don't need money. Everyone works as they can, everyone has equal access to food, medicine, housing.

A woman approaches shyly and hands her pass to Murgatroyd. "I almost didn't make my taxi on time," she says, and her voice is so pleasant, Murgatroyd stares. The woman's face is glowing, thrilled. She looks all around the ship, the doors to the lift, at Murgatroyd herself. "I couldn't find my toothbrush and I didn't know if they'd have any onboard. I'm so excited," the woman says. "I'm sorry I'm babbling." She smiles. "My name is Jenna."

Jenna is dressed casually in jeans and what looks like a handknit sweater. She's carrying a backpack and nothing else. Lower decks, for sure. Murgatroyd likes her already and can't wait to get to know her during the long hours ahead of them. Murgatroyd scans Jenna's pass and frowns. Upper decks. It can't be. She scans it again. The woman is a librarian, Murgatroyd reads on the scanner. "Upper decks?" Murgatroyd almost chokes on the words.

The woman smiles again. She meets Murgatroyd's eyes; her gaze is soft and kind. Murgatroyd wants to grab her, throw her in the lower deck's lift. This woman does not belong on the upper decks. "How did you..." Murgatroyd pauses, not sure how to ask the question.

"How did a librarian get to the upper decks?" The woman laughs. "We wanted to make sure all our favorite books were going to New Earth. So, when the lottery pulled my name to make the trip, most of the libraries on the planet donated to pay for my passage."

"You can petition to have certain books taken in cargo," Murgatroyd says. "You didn't have to pay for the upper deck passage."

"This way, we'll never have to worry about a shortage of books." She shrugs, looking sheepish. "I know your company is doing your best. But I don't know. I guess we wanted to make sure nothing was left behind."

The company has digitally scanned every book to date and they update the collection every time they come back to Earth. This woman, all her colleagues, what had they given up to bring a storage bay worth of paper books to their new planet? Murgatroyd stares down at the scanner, frantically thinking. She can't let this kind woman go among the vultures in the upper decks. "Listen," she says. "Your room isn't ready yet. I'm going to send you down to the lower decks just to wait. I'll come get you when it's ready."

The woman looks at Murgatroyd with trusting eyes. "Okay. Thank you."

From the lower decks, passengers can't access the upper decks without a pass. When the lift doors close on the woman, Murgatroyd keys in a new designation, lifting the upper deck privileges from the librarian. Later, Murgatroyd will find her in the mess hall and explain. Somehow, she'll try to make her understand.

Tonight, on the ship, the upper-class passengers will talk about how they're going to take over when they get to New Earth, and put some order back into the socialist nightmare Murgatroyd's company has created. She's heard it hundreds of times. Rumors have filtered back to Earth about the social order of New Earth and a lot of people make the trip just to change the way things are. Tonight, they'll tell her all about it when she stops in to bring them a complimentary bottle of champagne and chocolate-covered strawberries.

Murgatroyd just smiles and lets them have their dreams. They spread out on the upper decks, drink their free champagne, and barely spare a thought for the poor folks down in the lower decks, crammed into the bunks below.

They have it so good, Murgatroyd thinks, grinning to herself. But she'd been working on this ship since the early days, and she was there when the elderly billionaire from that online shopping company froze to death as they passed the third moon of Regulas Major.

The ship's engines keep the lower decks warm, too warm, maybe, but no one had ever frozen to death on the lower decks. No one ever died of asphyxiation on the lower decks, either, like four upper-decks people did when a bulkhead broke open on Murgatroyd's second flight. A class action lawsuit disappeared. In space, no one can hear you scream and that goes double for lawyers.

After the first couple of years, it became more expedient to simply dump the upper decks once the ship got far enough away from Earth. Less fuel, nicer people. The new planet was shaping up fine. Another three years of service, and Murgatroyd would settle there herself, riding on the lower decks, of course. Perhaps she'd adopt a dog.

The line moves on and Murgatroyd directs people to their appropriate stations. A leering man pinches her butt as he passes and Murgatroyd fakes a smile. "How about a free upgrade to first class," she says. "A cabin has just opened."

UNBRIDLED

Janet Richards

A flurry of chaotic curls
the perfect crown
Murgatroyd draws me in
as I knew she would

A movable energy
shifts between us
her unbridled compassion
our common passions

Murgatroyd gives me courage
to express the intimate
her voice spills unwavering
hard and soft truths

Some of us travel
gather pieces and leave traces
we fill spaces for a time
with our breath and our bodies

Crossed paths or kismet
Murgatroyd makes me smile
there is joy in spontaneous embrace
and the piece of her I still carry.

Author Biographies

Shawn L. Bird lives in the beautiful Shuswap Region of BC where she enjoys a retirement of writing and publishing. Her novella *Murdering Mr. Edwards* was nominated for an Arthur Ellis Crime Writing Award. Visit her website at ShawnBird.com

Laurène Boutin. With a lifelong passion for writing, Laurène, now retired, continues to pen narratives both in English and in French. Bull Mountain, tall and magnificent before her writing window, is where she finds inspiration. Between stories, you'll find her lost inside a book, or busy in her country kitchen, or at work in her gardens where beauty flourishes.

Finnian Burnett's work explores the intersections of the human body, mental health, and gender identity. They are a recipient of a Canada Council for the Arts grant and a finalist in the 2023 CBC nonfiction prize. When not writing or teaching, Finnian enjoys Star Trek and cat memes. Finnian can be found at www.finnburnett.com

Sherry Cassells writes the kind of short stories she longs for and can rarely find. Her stories have been published in magazines, anthologies, online journals and presses. She was nominated for a Pushcart Prize in 2022.

Renee Cronley is a writer from Manitoba that stepped away from nursing to prioritize her children, and has been channeling her knowledge and experiences into a poetry book about nursing burnout. Renee can be found at https://www.reneecronley.com/

Robyn Diner teaches Literature at Vanier College in Montréal, Canada. She's working on a collection of short stories titled *BadassTeacherLady: Tales From the Classroom and Beyond*. Her publications to date are a mashup of the personal, theoretical and literary, featured in journals such as: *DisComfort Zones*, *Liminalities*, and *thirdspace*.

Susan Duffield-Lodge Susan currently resides in Southwestern Ontario with her husband and English Springer Spaniel. She enjoys long walks along the Avon River. She was on the shortlist for a piece she wrote for BlankSpaces and also received 'Honourable Mentions' for two pieces published by OffTopic.

Lindsey Harrington is an Atlantic Canadian writer who enjoys exploring societal issues through a personal lens across media and genres. She has longlisted for the CBC Nonfiction Prize and shortlisted for the *Fiddlehead* Nonfiction Prize. She's currently querying her unmotherhood memoir.

Trevor Hodges spent 32 years as a teacher and school principal in the New South Wales Department of Education. After retiring in 2018 he took up writing full time. He's working toward publishing his first novel *Seeing Colours*, a Young Adult coming of age story set in a small rural school, in the second half of 2025.

Zilla Jones is an African-Canadian writer from Treaty 1 (Winnipeg) She is a Journey Prize winner and a finalist for the Bronwen Wallace award and the CBC short story contest. Her short stories appear in *EVENT, Prairie Fire, Grain, Prism, the Malahat Review* and others. Her debut novel, *The World So Wide*, will be released by Cormorant Books in April 2025.

Alma Lee is an artist living life and still in love with most of it. She is mother, grandmother, sister born in the boreal forest and determined to die in the boreal forest. She was partner of 34 years to a fabulous human whose only fault was that he passed away far too early.

Lavinia Leon is a Romanian-Canadian living in Alberta. She was recently longlisted for *Pulp Literature's* 2024 Magpie Award for Poetry, and her story "Lullaby for Seventeen of Green" received an Honourable Mention in Off Topic Publishing's Contest – December 2023. Lavinia can sometimes be found dreaming at lavinialeon.com.

Trent Lewin is a BIPOC writer of East Indian origin, an immigrant to Canada and a climate advocate, that has been published by *Boulevard, december, Grain, FreeFall* and *Ex-Puritan*. Trent is hard at work on two novels and numerous short stories. You can find his writing history at trentlewin.com/about.

Tom McCann began writing as a form of self-entertainment and for cathartic purposes. He is constantly trying to improve the quality and variety of his work. Although he has no compulsive need to be published he does hope someday to have written something of a quality that a traditional publisher is interested in.

Robert Runté is Senior Editor with EssentialEdits.ca. A former professor, he has won three Aurora Awards for his literary criticism and currently reviews for the *Ottawa Review of Books*. His own fiction has been published over 100 times. Robert lives in Lethbridge, Alberta, with his wife, two daughters, and four dogs.

Donnalynn Rainey studies literature in Quebec, and spends her days waiting for them to figure out she is a fraud. Until then, she hides out in the library gleefully absorbing knowledge; eats too many custard tarts; and pretends she's in charge of her cats. A delusion they graciously allow. For now.

Janet Richards lives and writes in the Bay of Quinte area of Ontario. A former newspaper reporter and editor, she has written creativity since childhood.

M. Gail Stelter is a retired school principal who authors Writing on the Senior Side, published twice monthly in a local newspaper. She has published two stories in *The New Canadian Stories Magazine* and ten others on curatedmicrofiction.com. Gail is completing a Certificate in Creative Writing at the University of Toronto.

T.L. Tomljanovic dabbles in drabbles, micro, and flash fiction writing from Langley, BC. Her work has appeared in *Carousel Magazine*, *Blank Spaces Magazine*, *The Globe and Mail*, *Every Day Fiction*, and Off Topic Publishing. Find her on Blue Sky @tomljanovic.bsky.social and at tomljanovic.wordpress.com/.

If you enjoyed this book,

please leave a review

at your favourite retailer.

You're invited to check out

these other books

from Lintusen Press!

PLATYPUS TALES
Short stories celebrating the oddly unexpected

A quartet of stories celebrating the delightfully odd, from Finnian Burnett, Chris McMahen. Shawn L. Bird, and Janet Whitehead.

GHOSTLY

13 tales from beyond the veil

A collection of haunting short stories from Alix Kelinda, Finnian Burnett, Halli Reid, Jarrod K Williams, Jeanna Mason Stay, Kaitlyn Petry, L. N. Hunter, Lee F. Patrick, Leslie Wibberley, Marie Powell, Rob Nisbet, Shawn L. Bird, and Theric Jepson.

THE DRAGON PROBLEM
a collaborative novel

The village of Zos has a dragon problem.
Follow the townsfolk as they deal with an evil dentist, a decrepit
dragon, a musical milkmaid, and political shenanigans.

A roomful of authors brainstormed this novel at When Words
Collide Writers' Conference in 2023 and 10 authors worked
together in subsequent months to craft this entertaining tale.

NEW SPACES:
an anthology of sci-fi short stories

Within your mind and across the universe, there are new spaces to explore!

From Lintusen Press comes this collection of ten science fiction short stories from authors Finnian Burnett, Andrew G. Cooper, J. Paul Cooper, BC Deeks, Nancy Kilpatrick, Philip Mann, Lee F. Patrick, Halli Reid, KT Wagner, and Jarrod K. Williams.

LINTUSEN PRESS
presents

small shifts
short stories of fantastical transformation

SMALL SHIFTS:
short stories of fantastical transformation

Not all shifters turn into magnificent beasts. Sure, there are those humans who transform into wolves and bears, but this book is about the smaller creatures. Learn about the trials and tribulations of folks who turn into raccoons, hamsters, mosquitoes, or bumblebees. 11 delightful tales of Small Shifts.

THE DRABBLE ADVENT CALENDAR

A drabble is a story of precisely one hundred words. Here are 25 family friendly winter themed drabbles; one perfectly complete tidbit of story to savour each day leading up to Christmas from authors Carol Parchewsky, Chris McMahen, Finnian Burnett, Lee F. Patrick, Shawn L. Bird, and Tim Reynolds.

Please visit

LintusenPress.ca

to learn more about our upcoming releases

and to see submission calls

for our future publications.

Thank you for leaving a review

on your favourite site or retailer

if you enjoyed this book.